PORNOGRAFIA

Other Works by Witold Gombrowicz

Ferdydurke

Cosmos

Trans-Atlantyk

Possessed

A Guide to Philosophy in Six Hours and Fifteen Minutes

Bacacay

A Kind of Testament

Diary

Polish Memories

Marriage

Ivona, Princess Burgunda

Operetta

PORNOGRAFIA

Witold Gombrowicz

Translated from the Polish
by

Danuta Borchardt

Grove Press
New York

Copyright © 1966 by Witold Gombrowicz
Translation copyright © 2009 by Danuta Borchardt
Foreword copyright © 2009 by Sam Lipsyte

All rights reserved. No part of this book may be reproduced in any form or by any electronic or mechanical means, or the facilitation thereof, including information storage and retrieval systems,without permission in writing from the publisher, except by a reviewer, who may quote brief passages in a review. Any member of educational institutions wishing to photocopy part or all of the work for classroom use, or publishers who would like to obtain permission to include the work in an anthology, should send their inquiries to Grove/Atlantic, Inc., 841 Broadway, New York, NY 10003.

Originally published in the Polish language by Instytut Literacki (Kultura) in Paris, France, under the title *Pornografia,* copyright © 1960.

First Grove Press edition published in 1978, together with *Ferdydurke.*

Published simultaneaously in Canada
Printed in the United States of America

FIRST EDITION

ISBN-13: 978-0-8021-1925-4

This publication has been funded by the
Book Institute–the ©POLAND Translation Program

Grove Press
an imprint of Grove/Atlantic, Inc.
841 Broadway
New York, NY 10003

Distributed by Publishers Group West

www.groveatlantic.com

09 10 11 12 13 10 9 8 7 6 5 4 3 2 1

Foreword

by Sam Lipsyte

The story sounds like the set-up for a very dark joke. It is 1939, the eve of Hitler's invasion of Poland. Somewhat oblivious to the coming catastrophe (like most everyone else), a writer from Warsaw accepts an invitation for an ocean cruise to South America. He'll be back in a few months, refreshed for his next project. But once he sets sail there is a slight problem with his itinerary: World War Two. Trapped in Buenos Aires with little money and no Spanish, the writer forges a life there for over two decades. Though he eventually returns to Europe, he never sees Poland, the country that formed (and infuriated) him, again.

Such was the odd fate of Witold Gombrowicz, one of the major writers of the modern age, though readers in the United States have not heard enough about him. International acclaim came late to Gombrowicz, with the French translation of his first published novel, *Ferdydurke* (1937). This masterpiece takes on more than a few literary forms in its hilarious skewering of European philosophy, cultural upheaval, and generational struggle. It remains one of the funniest books of an unfunny century.

Pornografia (1960), published over twenty years later, mirrors many of the earlier novel's themes, but in many ways it is a strikingly different work from *Ferdydurke*. It is also possibly a better one, tauter, its contents under more ferocious pressure, its savagery and comedy more directed. Narrated by a delightfully disturbing and nuanced man named (why not?) Witold Gombrowicz, *Pornografia* embraces an array of corrosive conflicts, between boys and girls, children and grown-ups, anarchy and the law, inferiority (life) and superiority (death), and competing versions of the real. (When the categories begin to deform and melt together, of course, things get truly, intriguingly, dicey.) Another opposition thrown into the pot is war and, if not peace, then a maddening state of not-yet-war. The latter seems especially important because *Pornografia* is set in a relatively calm pocket of Nazi-ravaged Poland, a place Gombrowicz never knew, and its plot consists of the erotic manipulations of a pair of would-be resistance fighters upon some increasingly witting farm teens. If that sounds like the makings of a gleefully tasteless farce, it might be because on a certain diabolical level *Pornografia* is one.

But it is also a profound behavioral study, though Gombrowicz eschews the staid tactics of some literary traditions, whose human specimens writhe under pins of omniscience. Here the psychology—the observations, projections, paradoxes, negations—belong to the panting insatiability of "Gombrowicz" himself, as he negotiates sexual devastation, poisonous and ecstatic social maneuvering, moral collapse, political ambivalence, and a country manor murder. The manic oscillations of this voice escort us into the wonderful, horrible core of the novel, a whirl of masks, duplicity, flesh and fragmentation.

It is a universe where an atheist must pray with true sincerity, deceiving even himself, to cover up the "immensity of his non-prayer," where a girl's hand is "naked with the nakedness not of a hand but of a knee emerging from under a dress," and where all human endeavor might just be a "monkey making faces in a vacuum."

Outlandish metaphors, syntactical bolo punches, arias of exquisite paranoia, these are not adornments in Gombrowicz, they are the essence of his style. His word play is deep play. "In the end a battle arises between you and your work," he wrote in his public diaries, "the same as that between a driver and the horses which are carrying him off. I cannot control the horses, but I must take care not to overturn the wagon on any of the sharp curves of the course."

Helping to keep the wagon upright here is Danuta Borchardt's brilliant new translation, the first in English from the original Polish. Borchardt's *Pornografia* honors both the wildness and the precision of Gombrowicz. She preserves his sudden and propulsive tense shifts and reveals a treasure of new cadences and swerves. Consider an older translation's description of the pious Amelia's sudden undoing in conversation with the novel's chief instigator, Fryderyk: "She was dumfounded (sic) and disarmed . . ." Borchardt's version is not only more vivid, but pivots on the weirdly compelling repetition of a word: "Knocked out of the game . . . she was like someone whose weapon had been knocked from her hand." Better still is Borchardt's Gombrowicz's take on nightfall. The older translation details ". . . the sudden expansion of the holes and corners that fills the thick flux of night." Fine, if a little vague, but it is no match for ". . . the intensification of nooks and crannies that the night's sauce was filling." The "night's sauce" is almost more than we deserve.

But it is never a matter of what we deserve. I certainly didn't deserve the gift of Gombrowicz when a good friend gave me *Ferdydurke* many years ago. I was just a young jerk who thought he had a fix on the frontiers of literature. But that book and others revealed the raucous speed and sublime vaudeville the right kind of runaway wagon could deliver. All who enter may revel in the many-layered excitements of *Pornografia,* though the reader is advised to refrain from slapping easy rejoinders to the existential difficulties the novel raises. "The primary task of creative literature is to rejuvenate our problems," said Gombrowicz in *A Kind of Testament,* a series of interviews with Dominique de Roux. And Gombrowicz did exactly that, through philosophy, satire, critique, all of it powered by a subtle and vicious comic prose that continues to offer dazzling views of our individual and collective derangements.

"I am a humorist, a joker, an acrobat, a provocateur," he once said. "My works turn double somersaults to please. I am a circus, lyricism, poetry, horror, riots, games—what more do you want?"

Let me know if you think of anything.

Acknowledgments

A translator does not work in a vacuum. I therefore want to share with the reader the names of those who with their works or in personal communications have informed my translations. You will find the list at the back of the book.

This is the third of Gombrowicz's novels, and most likely the last, that I have translated. Since there were omissions on my part in giving credit to those who are due, I would like to make amends. Beginning with John Felstiner and our translation group at Skidmore College in 1998, I want to go on expressing thanks to my friends Nona Porter and Alan and Barbara Braver whom I have buttonholed on many occasions. Professor Stanislaw Barańczak was the one who gave me the first impetus and encouragement to translate the first book—*Ferdydurke.* I had given Thom Lane previous credit, but this bears repeating. I want to thank him for his indefatigable assistance, as the native speaker of American English, in translating the three novels. His wide reading of literature and his keen intuition, since he knows no Polish, helped me to accurately express Gombrowicz's ideas. I am also most grateful to Alex Littlefield, my book editor, for his sensitivity in approaching this difficult and idiosyncratic text. Last but not least, my thanks go to Eric Price, the C.O.O. and Associate Publisher of Grove/Atlantic, Inc., for accepting my translation for publication.

Translator's Note

The first thing that strikes one about Witold Gombrowicz's book is its title, so I will open with the author's thoughts on its translation. In his conversation with Dominique de Roux in *A Kind of Testament,* Gombrowicz tells de Roux how he began writing the novel in Argentina: ". . . The year was 1955 . . . As usual, I began scribbling something on paper, with uncertainty, in ignorance, in terrible poverty that had visited all my beginnings. It slowly became rich, intense, and thus a new form emerged, a new work, a novel which I called *Pornografia.* At that time it wasn't such a bad title, today, in view of the excess of pornography, it sounds banal, and in a few languages it was changed to *Seduction.*" Perhaps when he chose to call his new work "Pornography," the word suggested something rare, hidden, a dark secret. I have left the title in Polish to convey shades of meaning the English may not have.

Since *Pornografia* has already been translated into English, the question arises why do it again. The simple answer is that the previous translation was from a French translation and not directly from the original Polish text. There are bound to be mistakes in any translation, but Gombrowicz's idiosyncratic and innovative use of language adds to the problem. Since the previous English translation was from an earlier translation into French, misunderstandings and errors were bound to multiply.

Let me give you a couple of examples of how far the earlier two-step translation had wandered from the original Polish. One of the central characters, Fryderyk, writes a letter to his companion, the narrator, in which he reveals how his somewhat twisted psyche operates. It is clear, from the Polish, that Fryderyk says: "I walk the line of *tensions,* do you understand? I walk the line of *excitements.*" The earlier translation has this as "I follow the lines of *force* . . . The lines of *desire.*" The meaning is quite different and, according to one expert on Gombrowicz*, this has led to a major philosophical misinterpretation of *Pornografia* by Hanjo Berressem and subsequently to that by Jacques-Marie-Émile Lacan. The reader may wish to investigate this issue.

Another example is from the ending of the book, which reads as follows: "I looked at our little couple. They were smiling. As the young do when faced with the difficulty of extricating themselves from a predicament. And for a second, they and we, in our catastrophe, looked into each others' eyes."

* Michał Paweł Markowski

The previous English translation presents this passage as: "I looked at our couple. They smiled. As the young always do when they are trying to get out of a scrape. And for a split second, all four of us smiled." The word "smiled" in the last sentence is incorrect, and the word "catastrophe" has been left out. The result is that Gombrowicz's ending, which is bizarre and striking, has lost much of its impact.

Here are a couple of examples of the way that Gombrowicz's linguistic idiosyncrasy has been lost in this two-step translation. The two main characters, Witold and Fryderyk, are riding on a train and Witold observes about Fryderyk: "and he just was! . . . and he just was and was!" The previous translation opts for the prosaic statement "but he remained there!" Another example is a condensation typical of Gombrowicz, where we are told: "the point is HENIA WITH KAROL," which the previous translation converts to a full sentence "in fact it is only about making: HENIA WITH KAROL."

A major piece of literature always has philosophical and psychological implications, and this is definitely true of *Pornografia.* To view it merely as entertainment or as a study on voyeurism would be a great mistake. There is no better way to convey this than by quoting the author himself, again from *A Kind of Testament*:

". . . The hero of this novel, Fryderyk, is a Christopher Columbus, setting out to discover unknown lands. What is he searching? Actually it is this beauty and new poetry, concealed between the adult and the boy. He is a poet of great, extreme consciousness, this is how I wanted him to be in the novel. But how difficult it is to understand each other these days! Some critics saw Satan in him, more or less, while others —mostly Anglo-Saxons—were satisfied with a more trivial label, *voyeur.* My Fryderyk is neither Satan nor a *voyeur,* but rather he has within him something of a stage director, even a chemist, who by bringing people together tries to create the alcohol of a new charm.

. . . [In this novel there is] a desperate fight of the adult wish for fulfillment with an easing-of-burden quality of youth that is light, reckless, irresponsible. A wish, that is the stronger the more it hits something that does not offer resistance. In the finale, the seventeen-year-old lightness deprives the criminals, the sins, of their importance, the novel ends in non-fulfillment."

Because of the novel's many levels of complexity, it is clearly important to convey the original with both clarity and faithfulness. A seamless translation would be wonderful, but it has been a challenge to achieve this while still leaving Gombrowicz's stylistic voice unscathed. It is my hope that my effort will lead to a greater appreciation and enjoyment of the novel.

—D.B.

PORNOGRAFIA

Information

Pornografia takes place in the Poland of the war years. Why? Partly because the atmosphere of war is most appropriate for it. Partly because it is very Polish—and perhaps it was initially conceived on the model of a cheap novel in the manner of Rodziewiczówna or Zarzycka (did this similarity disappear in its subsequent adaptation?). And partly just to be contrary—to suggest to the nation that its womb can accommodate conflicts, dramas, ideas other than those already theoretically established.

I do not know the wartime Poland. I did not witness it. After 1939 I never visited Poland. I wrote this as I imagined it. So it is an imaginary Poland—and don't worry that what I have written is sometimes crazy, sometimes perhaps fantastic, that is not its point and is of no significance at all to matters happening here.

One more thing. Let no one look for critical or ironic intent in the theme pertaining to the Underground Army (UA, in the second part). I want to assure the UA of my respect. I invented the situation—it could happen in any underground organization—because this is what was required by its composition and its spirit, somewhat melodramatic here. UA or no UA, people are people—it could happen anywhere when a leader is stricken with cowardice or when a murder is impelled by an underground resistance movement.

—W.G.

Part I

I

I'll tell you about yet another adventure of mine, probably one of the most disastrous. At the time—the year was 1943—I was living in what was once Poland and what was once Warsaw, at the rock-bottom of an accomplished fact. Silence. The thinned-out bunch of companions and friends from the former cafés—the Zodiac, the Ziemiańska, the Ipsu—would gather in an apartment on Krucza Street and there, drinking, we tried hard to go on as artists, writers, and thinkers . . . picking up our old, earlier conversations and disputes about art. . . . Hey, hey, hey, to this day I see us sitting or lying around in thick cigarette smoke, this one somewhat skeleton-like, that one scarred, and all shouting, screaming. So this one was shouting: God, another: art, a third: the nation, a fourth: the proletariat, and so we debated furiously, and it went on and on—God, art, nation, proletariat—but one day a middle-aged guy turned up, dark and lean, with an aquiline nose and, observing all due formality, he introduced himself to everyone individually. After which he hardly spoke.

He scrupulously thanked us for the glass of vodka we offered him—and no less scrupulously he said: "I would also like to ask you for a match . . ." Whereupon he waited for the match, and he waited . . . and, when given it, he proceeded to light his cigarette. In the meantime the discussion raged—God, proletariat, nation, art—while the stench was peeking into our nostrils. Someone asked: "Fryderyk, sir, what winds have blown you here?"—to which he instantly gave an exhaustive reply: "I learned from Madame Ewa that Piętak frequently comes here, therefore I dropped in, since I have four rabbit pelts and the sole of a shoe." And, to show that these were not empty words, he displayed the pelts, which had been wrapped in paper.

He was served tea, which he drank, but a piece of sugar remained on his little plate—so he reached for it to bring it to his mouth—but perhaps deeming this action not sufficiently justified, he withdrew his hand—yet withdrawing his hand was something even less justified—so he reached for the sugar again and ate it—but he probably ate it not so much for pleasure as merely for the sake of behaving properly . . . towards the sugar or towards us? . . . and wishing to erase this impression he coughed and, to justify the cough, he pulled out his handkerchief, but by now he didn't dare wipe his nose—so he just moved his leg. Moving his leg presented him, it seemed, with new complications, so he fell silent and sat stock-still. This singular behavior (because he did nothing but "behave", he incessantly "behaved") aroused my curiosity even then, on first meeting him, and in the ensuing months I became close to this man, who actually turned out to be someone not lacking refinement, he was someone with experience in the realm of art as well (at one time he was involved in the theater). I don't know . . . I don't know . . . suffice it to say that we both became involved in a little business that provided us with a livelihood. Well, yes, but this did not last long, because one day I received a letter, a letter from a person known as Hipolit, Hipolit S., a landowner from the Sandomierz region, suggesting that we visit him—Hipolit also mentioned that he would like to discuss some of his Warsaw affairs in which we could be helpful to him. "Supposedly it's peaceful here, nothing of note, but there are marauding bands, sometimes they attack, there's a loosening of conduct, you know. Come, both of you, we'll feel safer."

Travel there? The two of us? I was beset by misgivings, difficult to express, about the two of us traveling . . . because to take him there with me, to the countryside, so that he could continue his game, well . . . And his body, that body so . . . "peculiar"? . . . To travel with him and ignore his untiring "silently-shouting impropriety"? . . . To burden myself with someone so "compromised and, as a result, so compromising"? . . . To expose myself to the ridicule of this stubbornly conducted "dialogue" . . . with . . . with whom actually? . . . And his "knowledge," this knowledge of his about . . . ? And his cunning? And his ruses? Indeed, I didn't relish the idea, but on the other hand he was so isolated from us in that eternal game of his . . . so separate from our collective drama, so disconnected from the discussion "nation, God, proletariat, art" . . . that I found it restful, it gave me some relief. . . . At the same time he was so irreproachable, and calm, and circumspect! Let's go then, so much more pleasant for the two of us to go together! The outcome was that—we forced ourselves into a train compartment and bore our way into its crowded interior . . . until the train finally moved, grinding.

Three o'clock in the afternoon. Foggy. A hag's torso splitting Fryderyk in half, a child's leg riding onto his chin . . . and so he traveled . . . but he traveled, as always, correctly and with perfect manners. He was silent. I too was silent, the journey jerked us and threw us about, yet everything was as if set solid . . . but through a bit of the window I saw bluish-gray, sleeping fields that we rode into with a swaying rumble. . . . It was the same flat expanse I've seen so many times before, embraced by the horizon, the checkered land, a few trees flying by, a little house, outbuildings receding behind it . . . the same things as ever, things anticipated . . . Yet not the same! And not the same, just because the same! And unknown, and unintelligible, indeed, unfathomable, ungraspable! The child screamed, the hag sneezed . . .

The sour smell . . . The long-familiar, eternal wretchedness of a train ride, a stretch of sagging power lines, of a ditch, the sudden incursion of a tree into the window, a utility pole, a shed, the swift backward dash of everything, slipping away . . . while there, far, on the horizon a chimney or a hill . . . appeared and persisted for a long time, stubbornly, like a prevailing anxiety, a dominant anxiety . . . until, with a slow turning, it all fell into nothing. I had Fryderyk right in front of me, two other heads separating us, his head was close, close by, and I could see it—he was silent and riding on—while the presence of alien, brazen bodies, crawling and pressing on us, only deepened my tête-à-tête with him . . . without a word . . . so much so that, by the living God, I would have preferred not to be traveling with him, oh, that the idea of traveling together had never come to pass! Because, stuck in his corporality, he was one more body among other bodies, nothing more . . . but at the same time here he was . . . and somehow here he was, distinctly and unremittingly. . . . This was not to be dismissed—not to be discarded, disposed of, erased. Here he was in this crush and here he was. . . . And his ride, his onward rush in space, was beyond comparison with their ride—his was a much more significant ride, even sinister perhaps. . . .

From time to time he smiled at me and said something—probably just to make it bearable for me to be with him and make his presence less oppressive. I realized that pulling him out of the city, casting him onto these out-of-Warsaw spaces, was a risky undertaking . . . because, against the background of these expanses, his singular inner quality would necessarily resound more powerfully . . . and he himself knew it, since I had never seen him more subdued, insignificant. At a certain moment the dusk, the substance that consumes form, began gradually to erase him, and he became indistinct in the speeding and shaking train that was riding into the night, inducing nonexistence. Yet this did not weaken his presence, which became merely less accessible to the eye: he lurked behind the veil of nonseeing, still the same. Suddenly lights came on and pulled him back into the open, exposing his chin, the corners of his tightly drawn mouth, his ears. . . . He, nonetheless, did not twitch, he stood with his eyes fixed on a string that was swaying, and he just was! The train stopped again, somewhere behind me the shuffling of feet, the crowd reeling, something must be happening—and he just was and was! We begin moving, it's night outside, the locomotive flares out sparks, the compartments' journey becomes nocturnal—why on earth have I brought him with me? Why have I burdened myself with his company, which, instead of unburdening me, burdened me? The journey lasted many listless hours, interspersed with stops, until finally it became a journey for journey's sake, somnolent, stubborn, and so we rode until we reached Ćmielowo and, with our suitcases, we found ourselves on a footpath running along the train track, the train's disappearing string of cars in the clangor dying away. Then silence, a mysterious breeze, and stars. A cricket.

I, extricated from many hours of motion, of crowding, was suddenly set down on this little footpath—next to me Fryderyk, his coat on his arm, totally silent and standing—Where were we? What was this? I knew this area, the breeze was not foreign to me—but where were we? There, diagonally across, was the familiar building of the Ćmielowo train station and a few lamps shining, yet . . . where, on what planet, had we landed? Fryderyk stood next to me and just stood. We began to move toward the station, he behind me, and here are a carriage, horses, a coachman—the familiar carriage and the coachman's familiar raising of his cap, why then am I watching it all so stubbornly? . . . I climb up, Fryderyk after me, we ride, a sandy road by the light of a dark sky, the blackness of a tree or of a bush floats in from the sides, we drive into the village of Brzustowa, the boards glow with whitewash, a dog is barking . . . mysterious . . . in front of me the coachman's back . . . mysterious . . . and next to me this man who is silently, affably accompanying me. The invisible ground at times rocked our vehicle, at times shook it, while caverns of darkness, the thickening murkiness among the trees, obstructed our vision. I talked to the coachman just to hear my own voice:

"Well, how's it going? Is it peaceful over your way?"

And I heard him say:

"It's peaceful for the moment. There are gangs in the forests. . . . But nothing special lately. . . ."

The face invisible, the voice the same—yet not the same. In front of me only his back—and I was about to lean forward to look into the eyes of his back, but I stopped short . . . because Fryderyk . . . was indeed here, next to me. And he was immensely silent. With him next to me, I preferred not to look anyone in the face . . . because I suddenly realized that this something sitting next to me is radical in its silence, radical to the point of frenzy! Yes, he was an extremist! Reckless in the extreme! No, this was not an ordinary being but something more rapacious, strained by an extremity about which thus far I had no idea! So I preferred not to look in the face—of anyone, not even the coachman's, whose back weighed me down like a mountain, while the invisible earth rocked the carriage, shook it, and the surrounding darkness, sparkling with stars, sucked out all vision. The remainder of the journey passed without a word. We finally rolled into an avenue, the horses moved more briskly—then the gate, the caretaker, and the dogs—the locked house and the heavy grating of its unlocking—Hipolit with a lamp . . .

"Well, thank God you're here!"

Was it he or not? The bloated redness of his cheeks, bursting, struck me and repelled me. . . . He seemed to be generally bursting with edema, which made everything in him expand enormously and grow in all directions, the awful blubber of his body was like a volcano disgorging flesh . . . in knee boots, he stretched out his apocalyptic paws, and his eyes peeped from his body as if through a porthole. Yet he wanted to be close to me, he hugged me. He whispered bashfully:

"I'm all bloated . . . devil only knows . . . I've grown fat. From what? Probably from everything."

And looking at his thick fingers he repeated with boundless anguish, more softly, to himself:

"I've grown fat. From what? Probably from everything."

Then he bellowed:

"And this is my wife!"

Then he muttered for his own benefit:

"And this is my wife."

Then he screamed:

"And this is my Henia, Hennie, Hennie-girl!"

Then he repeated, to himself, barely audibly:

"And this is Henia, Hennie, Hennie-girl!"

He turned to us, hospitably, his manner refined: "How good of you to come, but please, Witold, introduce me to your friend . . ." He stopped, closed his eyes, and kept repeating . . . his lips moved. Fryderyk, courteous in the extreme, kissed the hand of the hostess, whose melancholy was embellished with a faraway smile, whose litheness fluttered lightly . . . and the whirl of connecting, introducing us into the house, sitting, conversing, drew us in—after that journey without end—the light of the lamp induced a dreamy mood. Supper, served by a butler. We were overcome with sleep. Vodka. Struggling against sleep, we tried to listen, to grasp, there was talk of aggravation by the Underground Army on the one hand, by the Germans on the other, by gangs, by the administration, by the Polish police, and seizures—talk of rampant fears and rapes . . . to which the shutters, secured with additional iron bars, bore witness, as did the blockading of side doors . . . the locking and bunging up with iron. "They burned down Sieniechów, they broke the legs of the overseer of the farm laborers in Rudniki, I had people here who were displaced from the Poznań region, what's worse, we know nothing of what's happening in Ostrowiec, in Bodzechów with its factory settlements, everybody's just waiting, ears to the ground, for the time being it's quiet, but everything will come crashing down when the front comes closer . . . Crashing down! Well, sir, there will be carnage, an eruption, ugly business! It will be an ugly business!" he bellowed and then muttered to himself, absorbed in thought:

"An ugly business."

And he bellowed:

"The worst of it is there's no place to run!"

And he whispered:

"The worst of it is there's no place to run!"

But here's the lamp. Supper. Sleepiness. Hipolit's enormousness besmeared with a thick sauce of sleep, the lady of the house is here as well, dissolving in her remoteness, and Fryderyk, and moths hitting the lamp, moths inside the lamp, moths around the lamp, and the stairs winding upward, a candle, I fall onto my bed, I'm falling asleep. The following day there's a triangle of sunlight on the wall. Someone's voice outside the window. I rose from my bed and opened the shutters. Morning.

II

Bouquets of trees forming graceful curving and curling paths, the garden was rolling gently beyond the linden trees where one could sense the hidden surface of a pond—oh, the greenery in the dappled, sun-sparkled dew! However, when we went out after breakfast into the courtyard—the white house, two-storied with dormer windows, framed by spruce trees and firs and arborvitae, footpaths and flowerbeds—the house overwhelmed us like an unspoiled vision from the now distant, prewar time . . . and in its untouched bygone state it seemed more real than our present time . . . while at the same moment the awareness that there was no truth to it, that it was inconsistent with reality, turned it into something akin to a stage set . . . so then this house, the park, the sky and the fields became both theater and truth. But here comes the lord of the manor, powerful, edematous, in a green jacket over his close-to-bursting body, and indeed he arrives as in the days gone by, greeting us from afar with his hand and he's asking if we slept well? Chatting lazily, without haste, we went through the gate, onto a field, and with a wide sweep of our eyes we took in the swelling and undulating land, all the while Hipolit prattling to Fryderyk about something, about the harvest, about the good crops, while crushing clods of dirt with his boot. We were now walking in the direction of the house. Madame Maria appeared on the porch and called out: good morning, while a little brat ran across the lawn, perhaps the cook's son? And so we moved about that morning—yet it was not so simple . . . because a kind of debility was creeping into the landscape, and again it seemed to me that everything, though still the same, was entirely different. What a disorienting thought, what an unpleasant, masked thought! Fryderyk walked next to me, in the light of this bright day, his body so real that one could count the hairs sticking out of his ears and all the flakes of his skin as pale as if he lived in a cellar—Fryderyk, I repeat, hunched, sickly, with sunken chest, with pince-nez, with the mouth of an excitable man, hands in his pockets—a typical city intellectual in a robust countryside . . . yet in this disparity the countryside was not the winner, the trees lost their self-confidence, the sky was blurry, the cow was not duly recalcitrant, the age-long past of the countryside was disconcerted, unsure of itself, as if tripped up . . . and Fryderyk was perhaps more real than the grass. More real? An irksome thought, disturbing, sordid, a bit hysterical, even provocative, insistent, destructive . . . and I didn't know whether it came from him, this thought, from Fryderyk, or was it the result of war, revolution, enemy occupation . . . perhaps one as well as the other, perhaps both together? But he was behaving impeccably when asking about the farm, conversing in the way one would have expected, and suddenly we saw Henia coming toward us across the lawn. The sun burned our skin. Our eyes were dry, our lips chapped. She said:

"Mother is ready. I ordered the horses harnessed."

"To church, to Mass, because it's Sunday," Hipolit explained. And he said softly to himself: "To church, to Mass."

He announced:

"If you gentlemen would like to come with us, you are most welcome, no pressure, merely broad-mindedness, ha, right?! I'm going because as long as I'm here, I'll go! While there is a church I'll go to church! And with the wife, the daughter, in the carriage—because I don't need to hide from anyone. Let them look at me. Let them gawk—as if I'm on camera . . . let them take photos!"

And he whispered: "Let them take photos!"

Fryderyk was already most obligingly offering our readiness to take part in the holy service. We are riding in the carriage whose wheels, sinking into the sandy tracks, are groaning dully—and when we ascended a hill, the expanse of the land appeared gradually, spreading low at its very bottom, below the tremendous heights of the sky, and it became solidified in immobile undulation. There, far away, was the railroad. I wanted to laugh. The carriage, horses, coachman, the hot aroma of leather and lacquer, the dust, the sun, the tiresome fly at my face and the groan of the rubber tires grinding into the sand—ah yes, familiar from time immemorial, and nothing, nothing at all has changed! But when we found ourselves at the top of the hill and felt the breath of the expanse at whose perimeter loomed the Swiętokrzyskie Mountains, this journey's duplicity almost struck me in the chest—because we appeared as if in a lithograph—like a lifeless photograph from an old family album—where a long-dead vehicle could be seen on this hill even from the farthest limits—and, as a result, the land became maliciously derisive, heartlessly disdainful. Thus the duplicity of this lifeless journey spread to the black-and-blue topography, passing us by almost imperceptibly under the influence and pressure of this very journey of ours. On the backseat next to Madame Maria, Fryderyk looked around and admired the colors, riding to church as if he were actually riding to church—he's probably never been so sociable and courteous! We drove down into the Grocholicki ravine where the village begins, where it's always muddy . . .

I remember (and this is not insignificant in terms of the events to be told later) that my dominant feeling was futility—and again, just as on the previous night, I would have leaned to look the coachman in the face, but this was not the proper thing to do . . . so we both stayed behind his inscrutable back, and our journey continued behind his back. We drove into the village of Grocholice, a little river on the left, while on the right, still sparsely set, were peasants' cottages and fences, a hen and a goose, a trough and a mud hole, a dog, a peasant or an old woman decked out for Sunday, strutting along a footpath to the church . . . the calm and sleepiness of this village . . . But it was as if our death was bending over a sheet of water, evoking its own image, our entry's past was reflecting itself in this eternal village and rumbling with frenzy—a frenzy that was merely a mask—that only served to hide something else . . . But what? Whatever the meaning . . . of war, of revolution, violence, debauchery, degradation, despair, hope, struggle, fury, screaming, murder, slavery, disgrace, lousy dying, of cursing or of blessing . . . whatever was the meaning, I say, it was too weak to break through the crystal of this idyll, and this little scene, long after its time, remained untouched, it was only a facade. . . . Fryderyk chatted with Madame Maria most courteously—or was he keeping up the conversation so as not to say *anything else*? We arrived at a wall surrounding the church and we began to dismount . . . but I no longer know what's what, what's it like . . . are the steps that we're climbing to the square at the front of the church ordinary steps or are they perhaps . . . ? Fryderyk gave Madame Maria his arm and, taking off his hat, he led her to the church entrance as people watched—but perhaps he did this so as not to do anything else?—while Hipolit rolled behind him and pushed forward with his big body, unwavering, steadfast, knowing full well that tomorrow they might slaughter him like a pig—he pushed with all his force, in spite of all their hatred, grim and resigned. The lord of the manor! However, was he, he too, the lord of the manor in order not to be something else?

But when the semidarkness, pierced with burning candles, engulfed us, the semidarkness that was filled with the stuffy air of a chant, plaintive, murmuring and resounding with this body of peasants, unleavened and stooping . . . then the lurking multiplicity of meanings vanished—as if a hand, more powerful than we were, had reestablished the dominant order of the holy service. Hipolit, until now the lord of the manor with his concealed rage and vehemence, anything but *to give in,* now soothed and noble, sat down in the patrons' bench and with a nod of his head greeted the land steward's family from Ikan sitting across from him. This was the moment before the Mass, people without their priest, the populace left to itself with its mawkish chanting, humble, thin, and awkward, yet holding itself in check—and so it was like a mongrel on a leash, harmless. What restraint, what soothing effect, what blissful relief, here, in this bygone era turned to stone, when a peasant became a peasant again, the lord—a lord, the Mass—a Mass, a stone—a stone, and everything was becoming itself again!

However, Fryderyk, who had seated himself next to Hipolit in the patrons' bench, slid to his knees . . . and this spoiled my peace somewhat, because he was perhaps exaggerating it a bit . . . and it was hard for me not to think that perhaps he slid onto his knees so as not to commit something that would not be sliding onto his knees. . . . But now the bells, the priest comes out with the chalice and, placing it on the altar, executes a bow. Bells. Suddenly a decisive element struck my being with such a force that I—exhausted, semiconscious—knelt down, this was a close call and—in my wild abandon—I would have prayed . . . But Fryderyk! I thought, I suspected, that Fryderyk, who after all had also knelt, would also be "praying"—I was even sure that, yes, knowing his terrors, he was not pretending but really "praying"—in the sense that he wanted not only to deceive others but to deceive himself as well. He was "praying" in relation to others and in relation to himself, but his prayer was only a screen covering up the immensity of his non-prayer . . . so this was an ejecting, an "eccentric" act that was taking him outside the church, into the boundless territory of total nonbelief—a refutation to the very core. So what was going on? What was about to happen? I had never experienced anything like it. I would never have believed that anything like this was possible. But—what happened? In fact—nothing. What actually happened was that a hand had removed all the content, all the meaning from the Mass—and here was the priest moving, genuflecting, walking from one end of the altar to the other, while the altar boys were hitting the bells and the smoke of the incense was rising, but the meaning was escaping from it all like gas from a balloon, and the Mass was collapsing in a terrible impotence . . . it was flagging . . . no longer capable of begetting life! And this loss of meaning was a murder committed on the periphery, outside ourselves, outside the Mass, by way of a voiceless yet lethal commentary delivered by someone looking on from the side. And the Mass could not defend itself against it, because it happened owing to some tangential interpretation, in fact no one in this church opposed the Mass, even Fryderyk connected with it most correctly . . . but if he was killing it, it was, so to speak, from the other side of the medal. His incidental commentary, his killing *glossa,* was a work of cruelty—the work of a harsh consciousness, cold, utterly penetrating, relentless . . . and I realized that introducing this man into the church was sheer madness, one should have kept him away from it all, for God's sake! The church was the most terrible place for him to be!

But what happened, happened. The process that had taken place arrived at reality *in crudo* . . . first and foremost it was the ruin of salvation and, as a result, nothing could save these boorish, fusty mugs, now extracted from any sanctifying mode and served up raw, like offal. This was no longer a "populace," these were no longer "peasants," these were not even "people," these were creatures such as . . . such as they were . . . and their dirt had been deprived of grace. But the unbridled anarchy of this fair-haired multihead was like the no less insolent shamelessness of our faces that had ceased to be "lordly" or "cultured" or "refined" and had become something glaringly themselves—caricatures that had been deprived of a model, no longer caricatures of "something," they were just themselves, and bare as an ass! And the mutual explosion of grotesqueness, of both the lordly and the boorish, converged in the gesture of the priest who was celebrating . . . what? What? Nothing. But that was not all . . .

The church ceased to be a church. A space had intruded, but a space that was cosmic, black, and this wasn't even happening on earth, but rather, the earth had transformed itself into a planet suspended in the universe, cosmos was here, this was happening somewhere on its territory, to such a degree that the light of the candles, and even the light of day penetrating the stained-glass windows, became as dark as night. Thus we were no longer in church, in this village, not even on earth, but instead—and in keeping with reality, yes, in keeping with the truth—we were somewhere in the cosmos, suspended with our candles and our glitter, and somewhere in that vastness we were performing these strange things with ourselves and among ourselves, like a monkey making faces in a vacuum. It was our particular teasing, somewhere, in a galaxy, a human provocation in darkness, a performance of bizarre movements in an abyss, grimacing in boundless immensity. And our drowning in space was accompanied by a horrible intensification of the concrete nature of things, we were in the cosmos, yet we were like something terrifyingly known, defined in every detail. The bells rang for the Elevation. Fryderyk kneeled.

This time his kneeling had a crushing effect, like killing a hen, and the Mass rolled on, though struck mortally and babbling like a madman. *Ite missa est.* And . . . oh, what triumph! What victory over the Mass! What pride! As if its abolition was, for me, a longed-for ending of sorts: finally I was alone, by myself, without anyone or anything but me, alone in absolute darkness . . . so I have reached my limit and attained darkness! The bitter end, the bitter taste of arriving and the bitter finish line! Yet it was all lofty, giddy, marked by the relentless maturity of the spirit, finally autonomous. But it was also terrible and, devoid of any resistance, I felt within that I was in the hands of a monster, and that I was capable of doing anything with myself, anything, anything! The insensitivity of pride. The chill of the outer limits. Severity and emptiness. What then? The holy service was coming to an end, I looked around sleepily, I was tired, oh, we'll have to leave, ride home, to Poworna, on the sandy road . . . but all of a sudden my gaze . . . my eyes. . . my eyes, panicky and heavy. Yes, something was pulling at me . . . eyes . . . and eyes. Captivatingly, temptingly—yes. But what? What was attracting and luring me? A marvel, as in a dream, shrouded places that we desire yet are unable to discern, and we circle around them with a mute cry, with an all-consuming longing that is heartbreaking, exultant, enchanted.

I circled around like this, still flustered, hesitant . . . yet already deliciously permeated by a lithe subjugation that was captivating me—enchanting—charming—tempting and conquering me—it sparkled—and the contrast between that night's cosmic chill and the gushing spring of bliss was so immeasurable that I thought dimly—it's God, and a miracle! God and a miracle!

What was it, though?

It was . . . part of a cheek and the nape of a neck . . . it belonged to someone standing in front of us, in the crowd, a few steps away . . .

Oh, I almost choked! It was . . .

(a boy)

(a boy)

And realizing that it was just (a boy), I began to rapidly retreat from my ecstasy. Because in fact I barely saw him, just a little ordinary skin—on the back of the neck and on the cheek. Then he moved abruptly, and this movement, imperceptible, pierced me through and through, like an extraordinary attraction!

And indeed (a boy).

And nothing but (a boy).

How embarrassing! An ordinary sixteen-year-old nape of a neck, with cropped hair, and the ordinary skin (of a boy), somewhat chapped, and (a youthful) position of the head—most ordinary—so what was the origin of my inner trembling? Oh . . . and now I saw the contour of the nose, the mouth, for he turned his face slightly to the left—there was nothing special, I saw in this slant the slanting face (of a boy)—an ordinary face! He was not a peasant. A student? An apprentice? An ordinary (young) face, untroubled, somewhat willful, friendly, meant for chewing pencils with his teeth, or for playing football, playing billiards, and the collar of the jacket was over the shirt collar, his nape was suntanned. Yet my heart was beating fast. And he exuded godliness, wonderfully enchanting and engaging as he was in the boundless emptiness of this night, he was a source of a breathing warmth and light. Grace. Unfathomable miracle: why did this insignificance become significant?

Fryderyk? Did Fryderyk know about it, or see it, did his eye catch it too? . . . But all at once people began moving, the Mass came to an end, a slow crowding toward the door ensued. And I with the others. Henia walked ahead of me, her back and her little nape still a schoolgirl's, and this is what came to mind, and when it did, it took hold of me so strongly—it linked up with the other neck so efficiently . . . that I suddenly understood, easily and without effort: this neck and the other neck. These two necks. The two necks were . . .

How so? What's this? It was as if the nape of her neck (the girl's) was taking a run for and uniting itself with (the boy's) neck, this neck as if taken by the scruff was taking the other neck by the scruff of the neck! Please forgive the awkwardness of these metaphors. I feel a little awkward talking about this—and also at some point I'll have to explain why I'm putting the words (boy) and (girl) in parentheses, yes, this too needs explaining. Her movement, as they walked ahead of me in the crowd, in the heated crush of people, was also somehow "relating" to him, and it was an ardent enhancement, a whisper added to his movement so close by, so close in this crowd. Really? Wasn't it an illusion? But suddenly I saw her hand hanging by her body, pressed into her body by the push of the crowd, and this pressed hand of hers was surrendering itself to his hands in intimacy and in the thicket of all those bodies glued together. Indeed, everything within her was "for him"! While he, farther on, calmly walking along with other people, was yet straining toward her, tensed by her. Oh, such a disinterested falling into love and desire, unheeding, blind, and moving on so calmly with the others! So! That's why!—I now knew the secret within him that, from the first moment, had carried me away.

We emerged from the church onto the sunlit square and people dispersed, while they—he and she—appeared before me in the fullness of their nature. She—in a light-colored blouse with a little white collar, in a navy blue skirt, standing to one side, waiting for her parents, closing her prayer book with a clasp. He . . . he went up to a wall and, standing on his toes, looked over to the other side—I didn't know why. Did they know each other? Yet, even though they each were separate, once again and now even more so, their passionate congruence hit the eye: they were here for each other. I narrowed my eyes—the square looked white, green, blue, warm—I narrowed my eyes. He was for her, she for him, even as they thus stood at a distance, not at all interested in each other—and this was so strong that his mouth matched not only her mouth but her whole body—and her body was subject to his legs!

I'm worried that perhaps I have truly gone too far in my last sentence . . . Shouldn't one rather say calmly that this was an exceptional *casus* of a good match . . . though perhaps not only sexual? It sometimes happens that when we see a couple we say: well, these two are quite a match—but in this case the match, if I may say so, was even more intense because it was not grown-up. . . . I really don't know if this is clear . . . and yet this juvenile sensuality was radiant with the treasure of a higher nature, namely, they were each other's happiness, they were precious and most significant to one another! And in this square, under this sun, muddleheaded and stupefied, I couldn't understand, it was beyond my comprehension, how it could be that they were not paying attention to one another, they were not striving toward each other! She was separate from him and he from her.

Sunday, the village, the heat, sleepy languor, the church, no one in a hurry, little groups formed, Madame Maria touching her face with the tip of her finger as if checking her complexion—Hipolit talking with the land steward about quotas—next to him Fryderyk, courteous, his hands in his jacket pockets, a guest . . . oh, this scene swept away the recent black abyss in which there had suddenly appeared such a hot little flame . . . but only one thing troubled me: had Fryderyk noticed it? Did he know?

Fryderyk?

Hipolit asked the land steward:

"And what about the potatoes? What shall we do?"

"We can give them half a meter."

The (boy) approached us. "And this is my Karol," said the steward and pushed him toward Fryderyk, who extended his hand. Karol greeted everyone, Henia said to her mother: "Look, Mrs. Gałecka has recovered!"

"Well, how about visiting the parish priest?" Hipolit asked and immediately mumbled: "What for?" Then he bellowed: "On with it, ladies and gentlemen, it's time to go home!" We say our good-byes to the steward. We mount the carriage and Karol, who has taken his place next to the coachman, is with us (what's this?), we're riding on, the rubber tires slipping into the ruts sound a dull groan, here is the sandy road in the trembling and lazy air, a golden fly is hovering—and when we have climbed a hill, rectangles of fields and a railroad track appear in the distance where the forest begins. We're riding on. Fryderyk, sitting next to Henia, hovers above the bluish-golden reflection of light typical of the local colors, the reflection—he explains—comes from particles of loess in the air. We're riding on.

III

The carriage moved on. Karol sat on the driver's seat, next to the coachman. She, in the front—and where her little head ended, there he began above her as if placed on an upper story, his back toward us, a slim contour, visible yet featureless—while his shirt billowed in the wind—and the combination of her face with the absence of his face, the complement of her seeing face with his unseeing back struck me with a dark, hot duality. . . . They were not unusually good-looking—neither he nor she—only as much as is appropriate for their age—but they were a beauty in their closed circle, in their mutual desire and rapture—something in which practically no one else had any right to take part. They were unto themselves—it was strictly between them. And especially because they were so (young). So I was not allowed to watch, I tried not to see it, but, with Fryderyk in front of me and sitting next to her on the small seat, I was again persistently asking myself: Had he seen this? Did he know anything? And I was lying in wait to see a single glance of his, one of those supposedly indifferent ones yet sliding by surreptitiously, greedily.

And the others? What did they know? It would be hard, however, to believe that something hitting you in the eye like this would have eluded the young girl's parents—so after lunch when I went with Hipolit to the cows, I brought the conversation around to Karol. However, I found it difficult to ask about (the boy) who, having driven me into such excitement, became my shame, while as far as Hipolit was concerned, he probably didn't think the subject worthy of his attention. Well, indeed, Karol, yes, not a bad lad, the steward's son, he served in the Underground, they sent him somewhere near Lublin, he got into some mischief there . . . eee, it was really stupid, he stole something, took a shot at someone, a colleague, or his commander, whatever, devil only knows, yah, nonsense, he beat it home from there, but since he, the rascal, is at odds with his father, they're at each other's throats, I took him into my place—he knows machines, makes for more people in the house, just in case. . . . "Just in case," he took delight in repeating it to himself, as he crushed dirt clods with the tip of his boot. And all of a sudden he began to talk about something else. Did the sixteen-year-old biography not carry sufficient weight as far as he was concerned? Or perhaps there was nothing to do but make light of those boyish pranks, so they wouldn't become too oppressive. Did he merely shoot, or shoot dead? I wondered. If he had shot dead, one could find him not guilty by reason of his being of an age that erases everything—and I asked whether Karol and Henia had known each other for long. "Since childhood," he replied slapping a cow's rump, and noted: "It's a Holstein! High milk yield! It's sick, goddamn it!" That was all I found out. And it appeared that both he and his wife had noticed nothing—nothing serious enough to have awakened their parental vigilance. How was it possible? And I thought, if the matter were more grown-up—less juvenile—if it were less boy-girl . . . but the matter was drowned in the insufficiency of their years.

Fryderyk? What had Fryderyk noticed? After church, after that butchering, strangling of the Mass, I had to know whether he knew anything about them—I could hardly bear his ignorance! It was terrible, that I could in no way unite the two states of spirit into one entity—the black one that had originated from him, from Fryderyk, and the fresh, passionate one that came from them—and these two states were separate, nonconfronted! Yet, if there was nothing between the two teenagers, what could Fryderyk have noticed? . . . And I thought it astounding, absurd, that they behaved as if there were no seduction between them! I waited in vain for them to finally give themselves away. Unbelievable indifference! I watched Karol during lunch. A child and a cad. An amiable murderer. A smiling slave. A young soldier. Hard softness. Cruel and even bloody fun and games. This child, still laughing, or rather still smiling, had already had his "shoulder put to the wheel" by grown men—he had the sternness and tranquillity of a youngster whom men had taken in at an early age, who had been thrown into war, brought up by the army—and, when he was buttering his bread, when he was eating, there was a noticeably peculiar restraint that hunger had taught him. His voice darkened at times, became flat. It had something in common with iron. With a leather strap and with a tree freshly felled. At first glance totally ordinary, calm and friendly, obedient, and eager as well. Torn between child and man (which made him at the same time innocently naive and relentlessly experienced), he was, nevertheless, neither one nor the other, he was a third possibility, namely, he was youth, inwardly violent, harsh youth that was handing him over to cruelty, to brute force and obedience, condemning him to slavery and humiliation. He was second-rate because young. Inferior because young. Sensuous because young. Carnal because young. Destructive because young. And in this youth of his—contemptible. But the most interesting thing was his smile, his most refined attribute, that actually connected him with degradation, because this child could not defend himself, disarmed by his own readiness to laugh. So then all this threw him onto Henia, as if onto a bitch, he was hot for her, and, indeed, this was not "love" at all but merely something brutally humiliating that was happening at his level—it was a "boyish" love in its total degradation. At the same time it was not love at all—and he really treated her like a young miss one knows "from childhood," their conversation was carefree and intimate. "What happened to your hand?" "I cut it opening a can." "Do you know that Mr. Roblecki is in Warsaw?" And nothing more, not even a gaze, nothing, just that—who, on this basis, could have accused them of even the most light-hearted love affair? As far as she was concerned, under his pressure (if I may express it this way), she was raped a *priori* (if this expression means anything at all) and, losing none of her virginity, indeed strengthening it even in the arms of his immaturity, she was actually mated with him in the darkness of his not quite yet masculine brute force. And one couldn't say about her that she "knows men" (the way one talks about dissolute young women), but only that she "knows the boy"—which was both more innocent and more licentious. That's what it looked like to me when they were eating their noodles. They ate those noodles like a couple who have known each other from childhood, who are used to each other, perhaps even bored with each other. Well then? How could I expect Fryderyk to see anything in this, wasn't it just an embarrassing illusion of mine? Thus the day passed. Dusk. Supper was served. We assembled again at the table bathed in the meager light of a single oil lamp, shutters closed, doors barricaded, we ate curdled milk and potatoes, Madame Maria touched the napkin rings with the tips of her fingers, Hipolit stuck his edematous face into the lamp. It was quiet—although beyond the walls that protected us the garden began, full of unfamiliar rustles and breezes, while farther on there were fields gone to weed because of the war—the conversation fell silent, and we were looking at the lamp, a moth was beating at it. Karol, in a corner where it was rather dark, was taking apart and cleaning a stable lamp. Suddenly Henia bent down to cut a thread with her teeth, she was sewing a blouse—and this sudden bending and clenching of her teeth was enough for Karol, sitting in the corner, to blossom and turn hot, though he didn't even budge. While she, putting the blouse aside, placed her hand on the table, and now this hand lay in the open, above reproach, decent in all respects, a schoolgirl's hand actually, still mommy's and daddy's property—and yet, at the same time, it was a hand laid bare and totally naked, naked with the nakedness not of a hand but of a knee emerging from under a dress . . . and actually barefoot . . . and with this licentiously schoolgirl hand she was teasing him, teasing him in a manner "stupidly young" (it's hard to call it anything else) yet brutal as well. And this brutality was accompanied by a low, wonderful chant that glowed somewhere within them or around them. Karol was cleaning the lamp. She was sitting. Fryderyk was arranging pellets of bread.

The doors to the porch barricaded—the shutters reinforced by iron bars—our coziness by the lamp, at the table, intensified by the threat of the unbridled expanse outside—objects, clock, wardrobe, shelf, seemed to live their own life—in this silence and warmth, their precocious carnality was also growing stronger, swollen with instinct and the night's business, creating its own atmosphere of excitement, a closed circle. It even seemed they yearned to attract the darkness of that other, the outdoor fury circling the fields, they needed it . . . even though they were calm, maybe even sleepy. Fryderyk was slowly putting out his cigarette on the saucer of an unfinished cup of tea, and he was taking a long time putting it out, unhurriedly, but when a dog barked somewhere in the barn—then his hand squashed the cigarette butt. With her slender fingers Madame Maria was enclosing the slim, delicate fingers of her other hand as one encloses an autumnal leaf, as one smells a wilted flower, Henia stirred . . . Karol also happened to stir . . . this motion, binding them together, burst forth, raged imperceptibly, and her white knees threw (the boy) onto his dark, dark, dark knees, his immobile knees in the corner. Hipolit's reddish-brown paws, thick with flesh, the paws that cast one back into antediluvian times, were also on the tablecloth, and he had to endure them because they were his.

"Let's get some sleep," he yawned. And he whispered: "Let's get some sleep."

Well, this was unbearable! Nothing, nothing! Nothing but my own pornography preying on them! And my fury at their bottomless stupidity—the kid, stupid as an ass, she an idiot goose! Because only stupidity could explain this nothing, nothing, nothing! . . . Oh, if only they were a few years older! But Karol sat in his corner, with that lantern of his, with his boyish hands and legs—and he had nothing else to do but to work on the lantern, concentrating on it, turning the screws—and, so what if his corner of the room was desired, precious, so what if great happiness was concealed there, within that not quite developed God! . . . He was tightening the screws.

While Henia was dozing at the table, with her weary hands . . . Nothing! How could it be? And Fryderyk, Fryderyk, what did Fryderyk know about it, putting out his cigarette, playing with the bread pellets? Fryderyk, Fryderyk, Fryderyk! Fryderyk, sitting here, seated at this table, in this house, in these nocturnal fields, in this swirl of fury! With his face that was one great provocation because it was, above all, steering clear of provocation. Fryderyk!

Henia's eyes were sleepy. She said good night. Soon thereafter Karol, having carefully wrapped the screws in a piece of paper, went to his room upstairs.

And then I said, trying to be cautious, looking at the lamp with its whirring kingdom of insects: "A nice couple!"

No one responded. Madame Maria touched a napkin with her fingers. "Henia," she said, "will be engaged any day, God willing."

Fryderyk, who went on rearranging the bread pellets, and not interrupting his activity, asked with polite interest:

"Really? To someone in the neighborhood?"

"Why, yes. . . . A neighbor. Vaclav Paszkowski from Ruda. Not far away. He drops in on us quite often. A very decent man. Extremely decent." She fluttered her fingers.

"A lawyer, mark you." Hipolit brightened up: "He was going to open an office before the war. . . . A gifted fellow, serious, a good head on his shoulders, quite so, educated! His mother, a widow, manages the affairs in Ruda, a first-rate estate, sixty acres, three miles from here."

"A model of saintly virtue."

"She's actually from southeastern Poland, née Trzeszewska, a relative of the Gołuchowskis."

"Henia is a bit young . . . but it would be hard to find a better candidate. He's a responsible man, gifted, exceptionally well-read, an intellect, you know, when he arrives here, gentlemen, you'll have someone to talk to."

"Unusually thoughtful. Noble-minded and upright. Exceptionally pure morally. He takes after his mother. An unusual woman, of deep faith, almost a saint—steadfast Catholic principles. Ruda is a moral mainstay for everyone."

"At least no mere riffraff. You always know what's what."

"At least we know who we're giving our daughter to."

"Thanks be to God!"

"Be that as it may. Henia will marry well. Be that as it may," Hipolit whispered to himself, suddenly becoming thoughtful.

IV

Nights passed smoothly, imperceptibly. Luckily I had a separate room, so I didn't have to put up with Fryderyk's sleep. . . . The open shutters revealed a bright day with little clouds above the bluish, dew-covered garden, the low sun pierced keenly from the side, everything was as if cast diagonally in a geometric, elongated view—a diagonal horse, a cone-shaped tree! Cute! Cute and amusing! Horizontal surfaces rose to the top, while verticals were diagonal! Such was the morning. Here I was, fevered and almost sick from yesterday's incandescence, from that fire and glitter—because one must understand, of course, that it all fell upon me unexpectedly, after those swinish years, stifled, debilitated, gray and madly twisted, during which I had almost forgotten what beauty is, during which there was nothing but the stench of cadavers. And now suddenly there blossoms before me the possibility of a hot, springtime idyll to which I have already said good-bye, and that reign of disgust gives way to a wonderful appetite for those two. I no longer wished for anything else! I was fed up with agony.

I, the Polish writer, I, Gombrowicz, ran after this will-o'-the-wisp as if after a lure—but what does Fryderyk know? My need to be sure if he knows, what he knows, what he's thinking, what he is imagining, became an outright torture, I could no longer be without him, or rather be with him, the unknown! Should I ask him? But how could I ask? How could I put it into words? Better still—leave him alone and watch him—see if he will accidentally give himself away by his own excitement. . . .

The opportunity arose when, following afternoon tea, the two of us sat on the porch—I began to yawn, I said I'd take a brief nap, but after I left I hid behind the curtains in the drawing room. This required a certain . . . no, not courage . . . daring . . . it had, after all, the character of a provocation—yet he himself had a lot in common with provocation, this was therefore a "provocateur's provocation." And hiding behind the curtain was on my part the first, clear breach of our association, the beginning of an illicit phase between us.

And besides, whenever I happened to look at him while he was busy with something else and he didn't return my glance with his glance, I felt as if I were committing a shameful deed—because he had become shameful. Nonetheless, I hid behind the curtain. He sat for quite a while on the bench as I had left him, his legs outstretched. He was looking at the trees.

He stirred, then rose. He proceeded to walk slowly around the courtyard, he circled it about three times . . . before he turned into a double row of trees that led into the park. I followed him at a distance so as not to lose sight of him. And I now thought I was on his trail.

Because Henia was in the orchard, by the potato field—was he possibly heading in that direction? No. He ventured into a side lane leading to a pond, he stopped by the water and looked, his countenance that of a visitor, a tourist. . . . So his strolling was merely a stroll—I was about to leave, gradually becoming certain that everything I had dreamed up was simply my fata morgana (because I thought this man should have a nose for this business, and therefore, if he hadn't sniffed it, it wasn't there)—when suddenly I noticed that he was returning to the double row of trees. I followed him.

He strode unhurriedly, stopped here and there, lost in thought, he looked at the bushes, his wise profile bending over the leaves, absentmindedly. The garden was quiet. My suspicions were being dispelled, but one poisonous one remained: he's pretending to himself. It seemed he was moving about the garden too much.

I was not mistaken. He turned twice more in various directions—deeper into the orchard—then moved on a bit, stood still—yawned—looked around . . . while she, about a hundred paces from him, on a pile of straw in front of a root cellar, was sorting potatoes! Astraddle a sack! He glanced at her fleetingly.

He yawned. Oh, this was truly unbelievable! What a masquerade! In front of whom? For what? This prudence . . . as if he were not allowing his own person to fully participate in what he was doing . . . but I could see that all this circling about was tending toward her, toward her! Oh . . . now he's going farther away in the direction of the house, yet no, he reappears in the fields far, far away, pausing, looking around, pretending it's a stroll . . . and yet, with a huge arc, he's aiming at the barn, and now, most definitely, he will go to the barn. Realizing this, I ran as fast as I could through the bushes to take up an observation post behind a shed and, as I sped to the sound of cracking sticks in the damp thicket by a ditch where they threw the cat carcasses, where frogs were jumping, I realized that I was admitting the thicket and the ditch into the secret of our little intrigues. I ran behind the shed. And there he stood, behind a wagon which they were loading with manure. Suddenly the horses pulled the wagon away, and he found himself facing Karol who, on the other side of the barn, by the carriage house, was looking at a piece of iron.

That's when he gave himself away. Exposed by the shift of the wagon, he lost his nerve because of the open space between him and his object—instead of standing calmly, he quickly skipped behind a fence so that Karol wouldn't see him—and he stood still, panting. But the sudden motion unmasked him, and so, alarmed, he rushed onto the road to return home. Here he met me face-to-face. And we walked toward each other along a straight line.

There was no room for hedging. I had caught him red-handed, and he—me. He saw the person who was spying on him. We advanced on each other and, I must confess, I felt uncomfortable, because now something had to radically change between us. I know that he knows, he knows that I know that he knows—danced around in my brain. There was still quite a distance separating us, when he called out:

"Ah, Mr. Witold, you've come out for some fresh air!"

It was said theatrically—the "ah, Mr. Witold" was claptrap on his lips, he never spoke like that. I replied bluntly:

"Indeed . . ."

He took me by the arm—he had never done this before—and again he said in a no less well-rounded manner:

"Oh, what an evening, and the trees are so fragrant! Perhaps we can avail ourselves of a pleasant stroll together?"

I replied with an equally minuet-like courtesy, because his tone was contagious:

"But of course, with the greatest pleasure, I find this quite delightful!"

We directed our walk toward the house. But this march was no longer an ordinary march . . . it was as if we were entering the garden in a new incarnation, with due ceremony, almost to the sound of music . . . and I suspected that I was in the talons of some decision of his. What happened to us? For the first time I sensed him as a malevolence, threatening me directly. He continued to hold me by the arm in a friendly manner, but his closeness was cynical and cold. We passed the house (while he continued to exalt in the "gamut of light and shadow" brought about by the sunset), and I realized that we were taking a shortcut, across the lawns, to her . . . to the girl . . . while the park, saturated with sheaves of glitter, was indeed both a bouquet and a luminous lantern, black with the firs and pines that spread wide, bristling. We were walking toward her. She looked at us. She was sitting on a sack, with a clasp knife! Fryderyk asked:

"Are we disturbing you?"

"Not at all. I'm done with the potatoes."

He bowed and said loudly, in a rounded manner:

"Can we therefore entreat this young lass to accompany us on our evening walk?"

She rose. She unbuttoned her apron. Such docility . . . it might, after all, be no more than courtesy. It was an ordinary invitation for a stroll, in a somewhat exaggerated tone, old-bachelor style . . . but . . . but in this way of coming up to her, of approaching her, there was, in my view, an indecency that one could define this way: "he's taking her with him to do something with her" and "she's going with him, so that he can do something with her."

Taking the shortest way, across the lawns, we headed for the barnyard, and she asked: "Are we going to the horses?" His goal, his obscure intention cut across the branching patterns of lanes and footpaths, trees and flowerbeds. He did not reply—and the fact that he provided no explanation while leading her somewhere became suspect again. A child . . . this was only a sixteen-year-old child . . . but here was the barnyard right in front of us, black, its slanting ground, encircled by the stable and the barns, with a row of maple trees by the fence, with the whiffletrees of wagons sticking out by the well . . . and a child, a child . . . but there by the carriage house the second youthful child who, while talking with the wheelwright, is holding a piece of iron in his hand, next to them a stack of boards, metal rods, and wood chips, close by a wagon with sacks and the aroma of chaff. We were approaching. Across the bulging, black incline. Having arrived, the three of us stopped.

The sun was setting, and a peculiar kind of visibility set in, bright yet dark—which made the trunk of a tree, the angle of a roof, a hole in the fence impressively and clearly themselves, manifest in every detail. The blackish-brown dirt of the barnyard spread as far as the sheds. Karol chatted about something with the wheelwright, slowly, country-style, an iron wheel in hand, leaning against a post that was supporting the small roof of the carriage house, and he didn't interrupt his conversation, he merely glanced at us. We stood with Henia, and suddenly this meeting acquired the meaning of our having brought her to him, especially since none of us spoke. And even more so because Henia didn't speak . . . her stillness released embarrassment. He put the iron wheel aside and approached us, but it wasn't quite clear whom he was approaching—us or Henia—and this created a kind of duality within him, an awkwardness, for an instant he looked confused—yet he stood next to us quite at ease, cheerful even, and youthful. However, because of our general awkwardness, the silence stretched for a few seconds more . . . and this allowed the crushing and strangling despair, the grief, and all the nostalgias of Fate, of Destiny, to swirl above them as in a ponderous, drifting dream. . . .

The bitterness, the longing, the beauty of his lean form now facing us—where did this come from if not from the fact that he was not yet a man? Because we had brought Henia to him, like a woman—to a man, while he was not one yet . . . he was not a full-grown male. He was not the lord. He was not the sovereign. He could not possess. Nothing could be his, he had no right to anything, he was the one to serve and yield—his leanness and litheness suddenly grew large in this barnyard, right next to the boards, the rods, while she responded to him in kind: with leanness and litheness. They suddenly united, but not as man and woman, but as something else, in their joint offering paid to an unknown Moloch, unable to possess one another, merely able to offer themselves—and their sexual matching suffered a dislocation in favor of some other matching, in favor of something more horrible but perhaps more beautiful. I repeat, all this happened in a matter of seconds. But actually nothing happened: we just stood. Fryderyk said, pointing to Karol's pants, a bit too long and covered with dirt:

"You need to have your pant legs rolled up."

"You're right," he said. He bent down.

Fryderyk said: "Wait. Wait a minute."

It was obvious that what he was about to say didn't come easily. He somehow placed himself sideways to them, looked straight ahead, and in a hoarse voice, yet very clearly, he said:

"No, wait. Let her roll them up."

He repeated: "Let her roll them up."

This was shameless—it was a forced entry into them—it was an admission that he was expecting some excitement from them, do it, you'll entertain me with this, and this is what I desire. . . . It was bringing them into the range of our lust, our dreams about them. Their silence swirled for one second. And for one second I waited for the result of Fryderyk's insolence, in this sideways stance of his. What happened next was smooth, obedient, and easy, so "easy" that it almost made my head spin, like an abyss noiselessly opening up in a level road.

She said nothing. She bent down, rolled up his pants, he didn't budge, the silence of their bodies was absolute.

Meanwhile the barnyard's bare expanse hit us with the whiffletrees jutting from the hay wagons, with a cracked trough, with the barn recently patched up that stood visible like a splotch in a circle of brown dirt and lumber.

Soon after that Fryderyk said: "Let's go!" We turned toward the house—he, Henia, and I. This happened brazenly and openly. In consequence of our turning back, our arrival by the carriage house achieved its sole objective—we had gone there so that she would roll up his pants, and we were now returning—Fryderyk, I, and she. The house with its windows, with two rows of windows, one below, one above, came into view—and its porch as well. We walked without saying anything.

We heard someone running across the lawn behind us, and Karol caught up and joined us. . . . He was still in motion, but he soon fell into step with us—he now walked calmly next to us, with us. His fevered breaking in upon us, on the run, was full of enthusiasm—aha, he liked our games, he was joining in—and his instantaneous transition from running into the silence of our return home meant that he understood the need for discretion. All around us a weakening of existence found its expression in the approaching night. We moved on in the dusk—Fryderyk, I, Henia, Karol—like some strange erotic combination, an eerie yet sensual quartet.

V

How did it happen? I wondered as I lay on a blanket, on the grass, the moist cold of the ground close to my face. How could it be? So she rolled up his pants? She did this because she was up for it, of course, nothing extraordinary, a simple favor . . . yet she knew what she was doing. She knew that this was meant for Fryderyk—for his pleasure—so she was acquiescing in his taking delight in her . . . in her, but not just in her . . . in him, in Karol. . . . Oh, indeed! She was aware then that the two of them can excite, seduce . . . at least as far as Fryderyk was concerned . . . and Karol knew it too, he had indeed taken part in this little game. . . . But in that case they were not as naive as it might seem! They were aware of their appeal! And they were aware of it in spite of their otherwise silly youth, because it's exactly youth that is better aware of it than maturity, they were experts in the elemental force which they inhabited, they possessed skill in the arena of their precocious bodies, of their precocious blood. But in that case why, in their relationship to each other, did they behave like children? Why so innocently? Since they were not innocent in relation to a third person? Since, in relation to a third person, they were so very sophisticated! But what worried me most was that the third person was none other than Fryderyk, he, so circumspect, so self-controlled! And here, all of a sudden was this march across the park, like a challenge, like the initiation of a campaign—his march with the girl to the boy! What was it? What could it be? And hadn't I provoked it all—by spying on him I had brought into the open his secret passion, he had been spotted in his secrecy—and now the beast of his secret longing, released from its cage, in union with my beast, was on the prowl! This is how things stood at the present moment, namely, the four of us were de facto partners, in silence, in this undeclared business, where any clarification would have been impossible to stomach—where shame was choking us.

Knees, hers-his, four knees, in pants, in a dress, (young) . . . In the afternoon, the previously announced Vaclav made his appearance. A handsome man! Without a doubt—a tall and elegant gentleman! Endowed with a fairly prominent yet delicate nose with lively nostrils, an olive gaze and a deep voice—a trimmed little mustache coddled itself below that sensitive nose, above his full and crimson lip. A type of masculine comeliness that pleases women . . . who admire the grandeur of form as well as the overly delicate details, the innervation, for instance, of the long-fingered hands with their fingernails cleared of cuticle. Who could cast doubt on his foot, high-bred, high-arched, in a yellow, tight-fitting shoe, and his ears too, shapely and smallish? And those little inlets of baldness above his brow that made him look more intellectual, weren't they interesting, even delightful? And what about the whiteness of his complexion, wasn't this a troubadour's whiteness? Truly, a striking gentleman! A winning patron! A refined lawyer! I hated him with my physical being from the very first moment with a hate mixed with disgust, a hate caught unawares by its own vehemence and conscious of its injustice—because he was, after all, full of charm and comme il faut. It was indeed not right and fair to find fault with such trivial imperfections as, let's say, a slight plumpness and roundness making their appearance on his cheeks and hands, playing in the vicinity of his belly—this too, after all, was refined. But perhaps it was the excessive and slightly lascivious refinement of his organs, his mouth overly adapted for tasting, his nose overly refined for smelling, his fingers skilled at touching—yet these were the very things that made him a lover! It is conceivable that I was put off by his incapacity for nakedness—because that body of his needed a collar, cuff links, a handkerchief, even a hat, it was a body in shoes, absolutely demanding these supplements of toiletry and tailoring. . . . But who knows, perhaps what annoyed me most was that he converted some of his faults, such as the onset of baldness, or his softness, into attributes of elegance and style. The carnality of an ordinary boor has the huge advantage that the boor pays no attention to it, and as a result, it doesn't annoy you, even if it's in conflict with the esthetic—but when a man takes care of himself, brings out, accentuates his carnality, picks at it, messes with it, then his every defect becomes deadly. However, where did I come by such sensitivity to the body? Whence came this passion for snooping, timid and unfriendly, as if from a hole in the corner?

In spite of it all, I must admit the newcomer behaved intelligently, even with class. He didn't puff himself up, said little and not too loudly. He was extremely affable. And his affability and his modesty were the result of excellent manners, but they were also bred into his unsuperficial nature, which was reflecting itself in his gaze and seemed to pronounce: I respect you, you respect me. No, he wasn't at all enchanted with himself. He was aware of his shortcomings, and he would surely have preferred to be different from the way he was—but he was himself in a reasonably cultured and wise manner, with dignity, and it seemed that, though he appeared to be soft and gentle, he was in fact uncompromising and even relentless. And all this bodily culture of his did not in the least originate from weakness but was the expression of some principle, possibly moral, he considered it his duty toward others, but it was also an expression of breeding, of style, something unyielding, well-defined. He had apparently decided to defend his values, such as refinement, gentleness, tenderness, and the more intensely history turned against them, the more intensely he defended them. His arrival produced changes, particularly in our little world. Hipolit seemed to get back on track, he gave up whispering to himself and pondering bitterly, it was as if he had been given permission to bring out of his closets his long-unused suits, and he paraded in them with pleasure—a stentorian, cheerfully hospitable country squire, with no reservations. "So how goes it? What's up? Vodka warms, vodka chills, vodka never bring you ills!" While the hostess too danced her ethereal lamentations and, waving her little fingers in all directions, she spread the shawl of her hospitality.

Fryderyk responded to Vaclav's respect with his own most profound respect, he let him pass through the door first, and only upon a slight hand motion from the other did he walk in first, as if submitting to his will—these were Versailles manners. There ensued a competition in courtesy, what was interesting, however, was that each of them extended his courtesy first and foremost to himself, not to the other. From Fryderyk's first words Vaclav realized he was dealing with someone exceptional, but he was too well-mannered to underscore it—however, the dignity that he ascribed to Fryderyk acted as a stimulant to the sense of his own dignity, he desired to be *à la hauteur,* and he treated himself with kid gloves. Fryderyk, taking on this aristocratic spirit with an unusual eagerness, also began to assume a haughty bearing—from time to time he partook in the conversation, but in the manner of someone whose silence would have been an undeserved catastrophe to everyone around him. And thus, all at once, his fear of incorrectness became his superiority and pride! As far as Henia (who was the real object of the visit) and Karol were concerned, they both suddenly dropped all *hauteur.* She sat on a chair under a window and became a docile young miss, while he looked like a brother assisting in his sister's courtship, furtively checking his hands to make sure they weren't dirty.

What a tea! Cakes and preserves found their way to the table! Then we went into the garden, where sun-filled peace reigned. The young couple walked ahead, Vaclav with Henia. We, the elders, behind, so as not to cramp their style . . . Hipolit and Madame Maria, both somewhat moved, slightly playful, I walked next to them with Fryderyk, who was telling us about Venice.

Vaclav was asking Henia about something, explaining something to her, while she, turning her little head toward him, attentive and friendly, was waving a blade of grass.

Karol was walking to one side on the grass, like a brother bored with his sister's being courted, he had nothing to do.

"A stroll like those before the war, . . ." I said to Madame Maria, and she fluttered her little hand. We were approaching the pond.

Yet Karol's dawdling about was slowly gaining force, intensifying, one could see that he didn't know what to do, his movements suggested that he was restraining his impatience, attenuated by boredom—and at the same time everything that Henia was saying to Vaclav began *to be* for Karol, even though her words were not reaching us—her whole way of being again imperceptibly united with (the boy), and it was actually happening behind her back, behind her, because she was not turning around, she didn't even know that Karol was accompanying us. And this, the almost fiancée-like conversation with Vaclav, suffered a sudden depreciation under the influence of (the boy) who was dragging behind her, while she herself began to twinkle with a perfidious meaning. The enamored attorney bent a hawthorn branch for her to break off, and at this moment she was most grateful, perhaps even moved—yet her reaction did not end with Vaclav but went on to Karol, where it became vacuously young, sixteen-year-old, stupidly frivolous, gadding about . . . and so there was a dragging down of feeling, diminishing its importance, converting it into an inferior, lowly kind, gaining reality at some lower level where she was the sixteen-year-old with a seventeen-year-old, in their joint deficiency, in their youth. We circled a copse of hazel trees by the pond, a hag came into view.

The hag was busy washing laundry in the pond, and when she saw us she stood up facing us and fixed her ogling eyes on us—a hag well into her years, a dumpy and bosomy slattern, rather disgusting, greasily rancid and filthy-oldish, with tiny eyes. She watched us, a wooden paddle in her hand.

Karol broke away from us, went to the hag as if he had something to say to her. And suddenly he pulled up her skirt. The whiteness of her underbelly lit up, as well as the black patch of hair! She screamed. The teenager added to this an indecent gesture and jumped back—then came back to us across the grass as if nothing had happened, while the infuriated hag fired abuse after him.

We said nothing to this. It was too unexpected, too jarring—a swinishness, brutally driven into us, legs astraddle . . . and now Karol was again walking with us, dawdling about, calm as could be. The couple Vaclav-Henia, deep in conversation, disappeared around a corner—perhaps they hadn't even noticed—while we followed them, Hipolit, Madame Maria somewhat startled, and Fryderyk . . . What's this? What's this? What happened? My bewilderment wasn't due to his having done this prank—the reason was that the prank, even though so jarring, became all at once of a different tonality, in another dimension, the most natural thing in the world. . . . And now Karol walked with us—full of charm even—with the strange charm of a teenager who pounced on old hags, with a charm that grew in my eyes, and the nature of which I did not understand. How could the swinishness with the hag bestow on him the splendor of such charm? Magic radiated from him that was inconceivable, while Fryderyk placed his hand on my shoulder and mumbled, almost inaudibly:

"Well, well!"

But right away he unwittingly rounded the word off into a sentence, which he enunciated aloud and without artificiality:

"Well, well, well, what's up, dear Mr. Witold?"

I replied:

"Nothing, nothing, Mr. Frydedryk."

Madame Maria turned to us.

"I'll show you a fine example of an American arborvitae. I planted it myself."

The point was not to disturb Henia and Vaclav. We were looking at the arborvitae when the groom appeared, running from the barnyard, signaling us. Hipolit went briskly ahead: "What's the matter?" "The Germans have arrived from Opatów"—indeed we could see some people in front of the barn—and, suddenly apoplectic, he ran on, his wife behind him. Fryderyk followed them, perhaps thinking that he could be of use, since he knew German well. As far as I was concerned I preferred, while it was still possible, not to be anywhere close to this, I was seized with weariness at the thought of the Germans, who were unavoidable, oppressive. What a curse . . . I returned to the house.

The house deserted, rooms empty from end to end, the furniture made itself known all the more in this emptiness, I waited . . . for the result of the Germans' visit soundlessly taking place in front of the barn . . . but my waiting slowly became a waiting for Henia and Vaclav, who had disappeared around the corner . . . and finally Fryderyk exploded within me in this empty house. Where was Fryderyk? What was he doing? He was with the Germans. Was he really with the Germans? Should I look for him somewhere else, by the pond, where we had left that girl of ours . . . that's where he was! Surely that's where he was! He had gone back there to snoop. But in that case, what did he see? Envy of everything he could see seized me. The emptiness of the house was pushing me, so I ran out, I ran supposedly to the barn where the Germans were, but I ran along the thicket behind the pond, along a trench into which frogs were jumping, making a fat, disgusting plop, and, having circled the pond, I saw them—Vaclav and Henia—on a little bench, at the far end of the garden, across from the meadows. It was getting dark, it was almost dark. And damp. Where was Fryderyk? He had to be here—and I was not mistaken—there, among the willows, in a recess, not clearly visible, he stood on guard under the bushes and watched. I didn't hesitate for a moment. I quietly worked my way to him and stood next to him, he didn't stir, I stood stock-still—while my showing up as an onlooker was a declaration that he had me for a comrade! On the bench their silhouettes loomed, and they were surely whispering something—but we couldn't hear them.

This was a betrayal—her base betrayal—she was snuggling up to the attorney, while (the boy), to whom she should be faithful, had been cast outside her ambit . . . and this tortured me as if the final possibility of beauty in this world of mine had been broken down by an invading decay, a demise, a torture, an atrocity. What baseness! Was he hugging her? Or holding her hands? What a disgusting and hateful place for her hands: in his palms! I suddenly felt, as it happens in a daydream, that I was close to a revelation and, as I turned around, I noticed something . . . something astounding.

Fryderyk was not alone, because next to him, a few steps away, almost totally concealed in the thicket, loomed Karol.

Karol's presence here? Next to Fryderyk? But how on earth had Fryderyk brought him here? Under what pretext? Nonetheless he was here, and I knew that he was here for Fryderyk, not for her—he had not come here out of his interest in what was happening on the bench, he came because he had been lured by Fryderyk's presence. Truly, this was as obscure as it was subtle. I don't know if I'll be able to put it into words. . . . I had the impression that (the boy) had turned up uninvited for the sole purpose of inflaming the situation even more . . . to make it resonate more powerfully . . . and more painfully for us. Most probably when Fryderyk, the older man, hurt by the young girl's betrayal, stood there gazing with his eyes fixed, he, the youth, noiselessly emerged from the thicket and stood next to him, saying nothing. This was wild and daring! But the dusk was enveloping us, indeed, we were almost invisible, and the stillness—none of us could say a word. Thus the vividness of this fact was drowning in the night's nonexistence and silence. And it must also be added that (the boy's) action had a smoothing-over, almost an exonerating quality, his lightness, leanness, gave absolution and, being (youthfully) pleasant, he could actually join everyone . . . (someday I'll explain the meaning of these parentheses) . . . And suddenly he walked away as easily as he had appeared.

Yet the ease of his joining us made the bench pierce us like a dagger. It was mad, incredible, (the boy's) joining us while (the girl) was betraying him! Situations in this world are written in code. Inscrutable at times is the configuration of people, and of phenomena in general. This, here . . . was terrifyingly expressive—nonetheless beyond understanding, beyond deciphering. In any case, the world swirled with strange meanings. At that moment a shot resounded from the direction of the barn. We all ran together, taking a shortcut, with no regard as to who was with whom. Vaclav ran next to me, Henia with Fryderyk. Fryderyk, who in critical moments became enterprising and quick-witted, turned behind a shed, and we followed him. We saw: nothing particularly frightening. A German, tipsy, was amusing himself by firing a shotgun at the pigeons—and soon the Germans scrambled into their vehicle and, waving good-bye, left. Hipolit looked at us, furious.

"Let me be."

His gaze leaned out of him, as if through a window, but he soon shut the doors and windows within himself. He went into the house.

In the evening at supper, red-faced and deeply moved, he poured vodka.

"Well, then? Let's drink to Vaclav's and Henia's health. They came to an understanding."

Fryderyk and I extended our congratulations.

VI

Alcohol. Schnapps. An inebriating adventure. An adventure like a shot of strong drink—one more jigger—though this was slippery drunkenness, each moment threatened a downfall into filth, into depravity, into sensual muck. Yet how could one not drink? In truth, drinking became our mental hygiene, everyone used whatever he could to stupefy himself, in any way he could—so did I—though I did try to salvage something of my dignity by preserving, in my drunken state, the demeanor of a researcher who, in spite of everything, keeps watching—who gets drunk in order to watch. So I watched.

The fiancé left us after breakfast. It was decided, however, that the day after tomorrow the entire household would go to Ruda.

Then Karol arrived at the porch in an open coach, a *britzka*. He was supposed to go to Ostrowiec for kerosene. I offered to accompany him.

And Fryderyk was just about to open his mouth and offer himself as a third—when he fell into one of his unexpected difficulties. . . . One never knew when this would happen. He was just about to open his mouth, then closed and opened it again—he remained, pale, in the claws of this tormenting prank, while Karol and I took off in the *britzka*.

The horses' trotting rumps, the sandy road, expansive vistas, slow circling around hills that were cropping up one behind the other. This morning, in this expanse, I with him, I next to him—both of us surfacing from the Poworna ravine, both of us visible, and my coarseness toward him was exposed to the jeopardy of being visible from afar.

I began thus: "Well, Karol, what were you up to with that hag yesterday, by the pond?"

He asked somewhat warily, to better gauge the nature of my question, "Why?"

"Everyone saw it, after all."

My opening remark was not precise—just to start a conversation. He laughed, just in case, to make it lighter. "Nothing to it," he said and cracked the whip, he didn't care. . . . Then I expressed my surprise: "If only she were good-looking! But she was the lowest of the low, and an old slut too!" Since he didn't answer, I stressed the point: "Do you go for old hags?"

He nonchalantly cracked his whip at a bush. Then, realizing that this was the appropriate response, he snapped the whip at the horses, and they jerked the *britzka*. His response was clear enough, though impossible to translate into words. We rode more briskly for some time. Then the horses slowed down and, when they did slow down, he smiled with a friendly flash of his teeth and said:

"What's the difference, old or young?"

He laughed.

This worried me. A slight shiver ran through me. I sat next to him. What did this mean? First of all one thing hit me in the eye: the immeasurable meaning of his teeth that were at play here, they were his inner whiteness, all-purifying—and so his teeth were more important than what he was saying—it seemed that he was talking for the sake of his teeth and because of his teeth—he could be saying any old thing because he was talking for pleasure, he himself was a game and a delight, he knew that his teeth, so high-spirited, would be forgiven every revulsion and disgust. Who was this, sitting next to me? Someone like myself? Not at all, it was a being essentially distinct and delightful, native to a blossoming land, he was full of a grace that was transforming itself into charm. A prince and a poem. Why then did the prince harass old hags? That was the question. Why did it amuse him? Was it his own desire that amused him? It amused him that, even as a prince, he was also in the throes of a hunger that made him desire even the ugliest of women—was it this that amused him? Was his beauty (connected to Henia) so devoid of self-respect that it was almost indifferent as to how it satisfied itself, and with whom it took up? Here darkness was being born. We went down a hill into the Grocholice ravine. I was discovering in him a kind of sacrilege carried out with satisfaction, and I knew that this was something that affected his very soul, indeed, it was something, in its very nature, desperate.

(It's possible, however, that I was devoting myself to those speculations merely to maintain, during the drinking, the semblance of a researcher.)

But perhaps he had pulled up the hag's skirt to show that he was a soldier? Wasn't this like a soldier?

I asked (changing the subject for the sake of propriety—I had to watch myself). "What do you fight with your father about?" He wavered, surprised, but he realized instantly that I must have heard it from Hipolit. He replied:

"Because he's harassing my mother. Won't let her be, the son of a bitch. If he weren't my father I'd . . ."

His response was beautifully balanced—he was able to confess to loving his mother because at the same time he was confessing to hating his father, this protected him from sentimentalism—but, since I wanted to press him to the wall, I asked directly: "You love you mother very much?"

"Of course! If mother . . ."

Which meant that there is nothing peculiar about it, because it's acceptable for a son to love his mother. Yet this was strange. Looking at it more closely, it was strange, because a moment ago he was pure anarchy throwing itself onto an old hag, while now he became conventional and subject to the law of filial love. So what did he believe in, anarchy or law? Yet, if he so obediently gave in to custom, it was not to add to his worth but to devalue himself, to turn the love of his mother into something commonplace and unimportant. Why did he always devalue himself? This thought was strangely alluring—why did he devalue himself? This thought was pure alcohol—why, with him, did each thought always have to be attractive or repulsive, always passionate and full of vitality? We were now climbing, beyond Grocholice, on the left there were banks of dirt, yellow, with cellar holes dug for potatoes. The horses went at a trot and—silence. Suddenly Karol became talkative: "Sir, could you find some work for me in Warsaw? How about in the black market? I could help out my mom a bit if I was earning money, because she needs it for medical treatment, as things are, my father just keeps carping that I don't have a job. I'm fed up with it!" He became talkative because these were material and practical matters, he could talk, and plenty, it was also natural that he was turning to me with this—and yet, was this so natural? Was this not just a pretext to "reach an understanding" with me, the older man, to come closer to me? Truly, in these difficult times a boy must gain the goodwill of older people who are more powerful than he, and he can achieve this only through personal charm. . . . But a boy's coquettishness is much more complicated than the coquettishness of a girl, whose sex comes to her aid . . . so this was surely a calculation, oh, an unconscious, an innocent one: he was simply turning to me for help, yet he was really concerned not about work in Warsaw, but rather to establish himself in the role of someone who needs to be taken care of, to break the ice . . . the rest will take care of itself. . . . Breaking the ice? But in what sense? And what was that "rest"? I knew, or rather, I suspected, that this was an attempt on the part of his boyishness to make contact with my maturity, and I knew from other sources that he was not averse to this, and that his hunger, his desire, made him approachable. . . . I went numb, sensing his hidden intention of drawing closer to me . . . as if his whole domain were to assault me. I don't know if I'm making myself clear. The association of a man with a boy is generally based on technical matters, protection, cooperation, but, when it becomes more direct, its drastic aspect turns out to be very noticeable indeed. I sensed that this human being wanted to conquer me with his youth, and this was as if I, an adult, were to succumb to irrevocable discredit.

But the word "youth" was not permissible to him—it was not proper for him to use it.

We had climbed a hill, and an unchanging view of the land appeared, rounded off by hills and swollen with its own immobile undulation in the slanting light that swirled here and there under the clouds.

"You'd better stay put here, with your parents. . . ." This sounded uncompromising because I spoke as his elder—and it actually allowed me to ask in the simplest way and as if continuing our dialogue: "Do you like Henia?"

This most difficult question fell so easily, and he too replied without difficulty.

"Of course I like her."

He said, pointing with his whip: "Do you see those bushes? They aren't bushes, they're the tops of trees in the ravine, in Lisiny, that connects with the Bodzechów forest. Sometimes there are gangs in there. . . ." He squinted at me, suggesting we were in collusion as to the meaning, and we continued on, passed a figurine of Christ, while I returned to the subject as if I had never left it. . . . A sudden calm, the cause of which I was not aware, allowed me to disregard the time that had elapsed.

"But you're not in love with her?"

This was a much more risky question—it was reaching to the heart of the matter—it could, in its obstinacy, betray my dark exultation, mine and Fryderyk's, which had began at their feet, at their feet, at their feet. . . . I felt as if I were touching a sleeping tiger. A groundless fear. "Naw . . . after all we've known each other since childhood! . . ." And this was said without a shadow of an arrière-pensée. . . . One might expect, however, that the recent event in front of the carriage house in which we had all been secret partners would make it somewhat difficult for him to answer.

Not in the least! Apparently the other was for him something in the background—and so now, with me, he was disconnected from the other—and his "naw," so drawn out, had the flavor of caprice and irresponsibility, even of roguery. He spat. By spitting he cast himself even more as a rogue, and all at once he laughed, his laughter was overpowering, as if it deprived him of the possibility of a different reaction, and he squinted at me, with humor:

"I'd rather make it with Madame Maria."

No! This could not be true! Madame Maria with her teary skinniness! So why did he say it? Was it because he had lifted the old hag's skirt? But why did he lift her skirt? . . . what absurdity, what a tiresome riddle. Yet I knew (and this was one of the canons of my knowledge of people gained from reading literature), that there are human actions, apparently nonsensical, that a man finds necessary because in some manner they define him—to give a simple example, someone may be ready to commit a useless act of folly simply not to feel like a coward. And who, more than the young, need to define themselves? . . . I was therefore more than certain that most of the actions or pronouncements of this green youth who sat next to me, with reins and whip, were just such actions "committed on himself"—one could even suppose that our, mine and Fryderyk's, hidden yet admiring gaze excited him in this game with himself more than he realized. Well, then: he went with us yesterday on that walk, he was bored, had nothing to do, he pulled up the hag's skirt to introduce a touch of debauchery that he perhaps fancied, for the sake of shifting from being the one who is desired to the one who desires. A boy's acrobatics. Well and good. But why was he now returning to this topic and confessing that he would prefer "making it" with Madame Maria, was there a more aggressive intention hidden here?

"Do you think I'm about to believe you?" I asked. "That you prefer Madame Maria to Henia? What nonsense!" I added. To which he replied with stubbornness, plain as day: "Well, I do."

Nonsense and a lie! But why, to what purpose? We were already approaching Bodzechów, we could now see the huge chimneys of the Ostrów plants in the distance. Why, why was he defending himself against Henia, why didn't he want Henia? I knew, yet I didn't know, I understood and didn't understand. Did his young age really prefer elders? Did he prefer to be with "the elders"? What was his idea, his aim—the awesomeness of it, its burning-hot sharpness, its dramatic aspect instantly threw me on the trail—because I, now in his domain, followed his excitement. Did this kid desire to roam around in our maturity? Of course—nothing is more common than for a boy to fall in love with a beautiful maiden, then everything develops along the lines of natural attraction. But, possibly, he wanted something . . . wider, bolder . . . he didn't want to be just "a boy with a young girl," but "a boy with adults," a boy who is breaking into adulthood . . . what a dark, perverted idea! But behind him were, after all, experiences from the arena of war and anarchy. I didn't really know him, I couldn't have known him, I didn't know what and how things had formed him, he was as unfathomable as this landscape—familiar yet unfamiliar—and I could be sure of only one thing, namely, that this scoundrel had left his swaddling clothes long ago. To enter into—what? This was exactly the unknown—it wasn't clear what or whom he fancied, so perhaps he wanted to play with us and not with Henia, and he was constantly letting us know that age should not be an obstacle. . . . How so? How so? Well, yes, he was bored, he wanted to have fun, to play at something he was unfamiliar with, something he hadn't actually thought about, out of boredom, by way of digression and without any effort . . . with us but not with Henia because, in our ugliness, we could lead him farther, we were more unrestricted. Therefore (considering that event in front of the carriage house) he was letting me know that he's not disgusted. . . . Enough. I was sickened at the very thought that his beauty sought my ugliness. I changed the subject.

"Do you go to church? Do you believe in God?"

A question calling for seriousness, a question protecting me from his treacherous levity.

"In God? Whatever the priests say, that . . ."

"But do you believe in God?"

"Sure. But . . ."

"But what?"

He fell silent.

I was going to ask: Do you go to church? Instead I asked: "Do you go whoring?"

"Sometimes."

"Are you popular with women?"

He laughed right away.

"No. Not at all! I'm still too young."

Too young. Its meaning was degrading—that was why this time he could use the word "youth" with ease. But, as far as I was concerned, God and this boy had all of a sudden combined with women in some kind of grotesque and almost drunken quid pro quo, his "too young" sounded strange, like a warning. Yes, too young in relation to a woman as much as to God, too young in relation to everything—and it wasn't important whether he believes or doesn't believe, whether he's popular with women or not, because he was "too young" in general, and none of his emotions, or his beliefs, or his word could have any meaning—he was incomplete, he was "too young." "Too young" in relation to Henia and to everything that was arising between them, and also "too young" in relation to Fryderyk and to me . . . What was then this slim, tender age of his? Karol meant nothing to me after all! How could I, an adult, place all my seriousness in his nonseriousness, to listen intently and with trembling to someone who was not serious? I looked around the countryside. From here, from the hilltop, I could already see Kamienna, and we could hear the barely audible rumble of the train that was approaching Bodzechów, the whole river valley was before us, and the highway too—while to the right and left was the yellow-green patchwork of the fields, and, as far as the eye could see, a sleepy age-long past, but now gagged, quashed, its yap muzzled. A strange odor of lawlessness permeated everything, and here I was, in this lawlessness, with this boy, who was "too young," a light-headed lightweight whose insufficiency, incompleteness became, under these conditions, the primary power. How was I, deprived of any buttress, to defend myself from him?

We drove onto the highway, and the *britzka* began to shake across the potholes, the iron rims of its wheels making a grinding sound, then more and more people, we passed them as they emerged walking along a pathway, this one wearing a cap, another a hat, farther along we came across a wagon full of bundles, someone's entire belongings—moving step by step—while farther on a woman standing in the middle of the road stopped us and came up to us, I saw a fairly refined face draped in the kind of scarf usually worn by countrywomen, her huge legs in men's knee-high boots sticking out from under a short, black silk skirt, she was dressed in a low décolletage, ballroom or evening gown style, elegant, and in her hand she held something wrapped in a newspaper—she began waving it—wanted to say something, but then she buttoned her lip, and again she wanted to say something, but instead she waved her hand, jumped aside—then continued to stand in the middle of the road as we moved away. Karol laughed. We finally reached Ostrowiec with a loud clatter, bouncing on the cobblestones that made even our cheeks shake, we passed German sentries in front of a factory, the little town was the same as ever, ever the same, chimneys of the huge furnaces of the factory piling up, the wall, farther on a bridge on the Kamienna, railroad tracks, and the main street leading to the market square, and on the corner was Malinowski's café. Just one thing, an absence that was palpable, namely, there were no Jews. There were, however, lots of people in the streets, hustle and bustle, quite animated in places, here an old woman throwing garbage from a hallway, there someone walking with a thick rope tucked under his arm, a small group in front of a food store, a little boy with a stone taking aim at a bird that had settled on top of a chimney. We bought a supply of kerosene and made a few other purchases, then we left this strange Ostrowiec, and when the soil of a simple dirt road received our *britzka* on its soft bosom again, we sighed with relief. But what was Fryderyk doing? How was he managing, left there to his own devices? Was he sleeping? Sitting? Walking? I certainly knew his meticulous attention to propriety, I knew that if he were sitting it would be with all precaution, yet I began to worry that I didn't know how he was actually spending his time. He wasn't there when, having arrived in Poworna, we sat down to a late lunch, then Madame Maria told me that he was hoeing. . . . What? He was hoeing a path in the garden. "I'm afraid . . . he's probably bored here," she added not without worry, as if he were a guest in prewar times, while Hipolit came to inform me as well:

"Your companion, mind you, is in the garden. . . . He's hoeing."

And something in his voice indicated that the man was beginning to be a burden to him—he was embarrassed, unhappy, and helpless. I went to Fryderyk. When he saw me, he put away the hoe, and with simple courtesy asked if our trip had been a success . . . then, his gaze cast sideways, he proposed the thought, carefully worded, that perhaps we should return to Warsaw, because, when all is said and done, we can't be of much help here, and a prolonged neglect of our other little business may end unfavorably, yes, actually this trip here had not been thought through enough, perhaps we should pack our bags . . . He was paving his way to a decision, he was imperceptibly making it stronger and stronger, getting himself . . . me, the neighboring trees, used to it. What did I think? Because, on the other hand and in spite of everything, it is better to be in the country . . . and yet . . . we could leave tomorrow, couldn't we? Suddenly his questioning sounded urgent, and I understood: he wanted to deduce from my response whether I had reached an understanding with Karol: he surmised that I must have probed Karol, now he wanted to know if there was a shadow of hope that Karol's boyish arms would some day embrace Vaclav's fiancée! And at the same time he was furtively letting me know that nothing he knew, nothing that he had looked into, entitled us to such illusions.

It's hard to describe the disgusting aspect of this scene. An older man's countenance is held up by a secret willpower aimed at masking his disintegration, or at least at organizing it into a pleasing whole—but in his case there was disappointment, he renounced magic, hope, passion, and all his wrinkles spread around and preyed on him as if on a corpse. He was meekly and humbly vile in the surrender to his own repulsiveness—and he infected me with his swinishness to such an extent that my own vermin swarmed within me, crept out and crawled all over me. However, this was not yet the pinnacle of revulsion. The ultimate grotesque horror came from the fact that we were like a couple of lovers, let down in our feelings and rejected by the other two lovers, and our aroused state, our excitement, had nowhere to discharge itself, so now it roamed between us . . . now there was nothing left except ourselves . . . and, disgusted with each other, we were still together in our awakened sensuality. That was why we tried not to look at each other. The sun was burning us, the stink of Spanish flies emanated from the bushes.

I finally understood, during this secret conference between us, what a blow the now doubtless indifference of the other two was to us. The young girl—as Vaclav's fiancée. The young boy—totally unconcerned by this. And everything drowned in their young blindness. The ruin of our dreams!

I replied to Fryderyk: who knows, perhaps our absence in Warsaw was not advisable. He latched on to this immediately. We were now under the sign of escape and, moving slowly along the alley, we were becoming used to this decision.

But around the corner of the house, on the sidewalk leading to the office, we happened upon them. She with a bottle in her hand. He in front of her—they were talking. Their childishness, their utter childishness, was obvious, she—a schoolgirl, he—a schoolboy and a kid.

Fryderyk asked them: "What are you up to?"

She: "The cork slipped inside the bottle."

Karol, holding up the bottle to the light: "I'll get it out with a piece of wire."

Fryderyk: "It's not so easy."

She: "Perhaps I'd better look for another cork."

Karol: "Don't worry . . . I'll get it out. . . ."

Fryderyk: "The neck is too narrow."

Karol: "As it went in, so it will come out."

She: "Or it'll crumble and mess the juice up even more."

Fryderyk didn't respond. Karol was rocking stupidly on his heels. She stood with the bottle. She said:

"I'll look for corks upstairs. There are none in the pantry."

Karol: "I'm telling you, I'll get it out."

Fryderyk: "It's not easy to get inside that neck."

She: "*Seek and ye shall find!*"

Karol: "You know what? How about those little bottles in the cabinet . . ."

She: "No. Those are medicine bottles."

Fryderyk: "Could be washed."

A bird flew by.

Fryderyk: "What kind of bird was that?"

Karol: "An oriole."

Fryderyk: "Are there a lot of them here?"

She: "Look what a big earthworm."

Karol kept rocking, his legs spread apart, she raised her leg to scratch her calf—but his shoe, resting just on the heel, rose, made a half-turn, and squashed the earthworm . . . just at one end, just as much as the reach of his foot allowed, because he didn't feel like lifting his heel from the ground, the rest of the worm's thorax began to stiffen and squirm, which he watched with interest. This would not have been any more important than a fly's throes of death on a flytrap or a moth's within the glass of a lamp—if Fryderyk's gaze, glassy, had not sucked itself onto that earthworm, extracting its suffering to the full. One could imagine that he would be indignant, but in truth there was nothing within him but penetration into torture, draining the chalice to the last drop. He hunted it, sucked it, caught it, took it in and—numb and mute, caught in the claws of pain—he was unable to move. Karol looked at him out of the corner of his eye but did not finish off the earthworm, he saw Fryderyk's horror as sheer hysterics. . . .

Henia's shoe moved forward and she crushed the worm.

But only from the opposite end, with great precision, saving the central part so that it could continue to squirm and twist.

All of it—was insignificant . . . as far as the crushing of a worm can be trivial and insignificant.

Karol: "Near Lvov there are more birds than here."

Henia: "I have to peel the potatoes."

Fryderyk: "I don't envy you. . . . It's a boring job."

As we were returning home we talked for a while, then Fryderyk disappeared somewhere, and I didn't know where he was—but I knew what he was into. He was thinking about what had just happened, about the thoughtless legs that had joined in the cruelty they committed jointly to the twitching body. Cruelty? Was it cruelty? More like something trivial, the trivial killing of a worm, just so, nonchalantly, because it had crawled under a shoe—oh, we kill so many worms! No, not cruelty, thoughtlessness rather, which, with children's eyes, watches the droll throes of death without feeling pain. It was a trifle. But for Fryderyk? To a discerning consciousness? To a sensibility that is cable of empathy? Wasn't this, for him, a bloodcurdling deed in its enormity—surely pain, suffering are as terrible in a worm's body as in the body of a giant, pain is "one" just as space is one, indivisible, wherever it appears, it is the same total horror. Thus for him this deed must have been, one could say, terrible, they had called forth torture, created pain, with the soles of their shoes they had changed the earth's peaceful existence into an existence that was hellish—one cannot imagine a more powerful crime, a greater sin. Sin . . . Sin . . . Yes, this was a sin—but, if a sin, it was a sin committed jointly—and their legs had united on the worm's twitching body. . . .

I knew what he was thinking, the crazy man! Crazy! He was thinking about them—he was thinking that they had crushed the worm "for him." "Don't be fooled. Don't believe that we don't have anything in common. . . . Surely you saw it, didn't you: one of us crushed . . . and the other one crushed . . . the worm. We did it for you. To unite ourselves—in front of you and for you—in sin."

This must have been Fryderyk's thought at this moment. Yet it's possible that I was suggesting my own idea to him. But who knows—perhaps at this moment he was, in the same way, suggesting to me his idea . . . and he was thinking about me in a way that was no different from the way I was thinking about him . . . so it's possible that each one of us was breeding his own idea by placing it in the other. This amused me, I laughed—and I thought that perhaps he too had laughed. . . .

"We did it for you to unite in sin in front of you." . . .

If they really wanted to convey to us this hidden meaning with their nimbly crushing legs . . . if that's what it was supposed to be . . . surely, no need to repeat it twice! A wise brain needs no twain! I again smiled at the thought that perhaps Fryderyk was smiling at this moment and thinking that I'm thinking the following about him: that any laborious decisions to depart have vanished from his head, that he is again like a hound on the trail, full of suddenly awakened hope, his blood roused.

Giddy hopes—perspectives—were indeed opening up that had been contained within the little word "sin." If this little boy and this little girl suddenly craved sin . . . with each other . . . but also with us . . . Oh, I could almost see Fryderyk sitting somewhere and thinking, his head resting on his hand—that sin pervades us at the deepest level of intimacy, bonding us no less than a hot caress, that sin is our common secret, private, clandestine, embarrassing, leading us as far into another person's existence as physical love leads into the body. If this were the case . . . then it would surely follow that he, Fryderyk ("that he, Witold"—thought Fryderyk) . . . well, that we both . . . are not too old for them—in other words, their youth is not inaccessible to us. What is the purpose of a sin committed jointly? It's as if sin is created to illegally marry a boy's florescence with a girl to someone . . . not so enticing . . . to someone older and more serious. I smiled again. They were, in their virtue, closed off from us, hermetic. But in sin, they could roll about with us. . . . That's what Fryderyk was thinking! And I almost saw him, a finger to his lips, looking for a sin that would let him chum up with them, looking for such a sin—or rather, perhaps he's thinking, perhaps he is suspecting that I am the one looking for such a sin. What a system of mirrors—I was a mirror for him, he for me—and so, spinning daydreams on each other's account, we were arriving at designs that neither of us would dare to consider as his own.

Next morning we were supposed to travel to Ruda. The expedition was the subject of detailed deliberations—which horses, what route, which vehicles. It so happened that I went with Henia in the *britzka*. Since Fryderyk didn't want to decide, we cast a coin and fate designated me as her companion. The morning was immense, its bearings lost, the road distant over the rising and falling of the undulating terrain with roads cut deep into it, their walls yellowish and sparsely adorned with a bush, a tree, a cow, while in front of us the carriage with Karol on the coach box appeared and disappeared. She—in her holiday best, her coat white from the dust and thrown over her shoulders—a fiancée traveling to her fiancé. And so, infuriated, after a few introductory sentences, I said: "My congratulations! You'll get married and start a family. You'll have children!" She replied:

"I'll have children."

She replied, but the way she said it! Obediently—fervently—like a schoolgirl. As if someone had taught her the lesson. As if, in relation to her own children, she herself had become an obedient child. We rode on. Horse tails in front of us and horse rumps too. Yes! She wanted to marry the attorney! She wanted to have children with him! And she was saying this while there, in front of us, was the outline of her underage lover's silhouette!

We passed a heap of rubble discarded on the side of the road, and soon thereafter two acacia trees.

"Do you like Karol?"

"Sure. . . after all, we've known each other. . ."

"I know. Since childhood. But I'm asking whether you feel anything for him?"

"Me? I like him a lot."

"'Like'? That's all. So why did you crush the worm with him?"

"What worm?"

"And what about the pants legs? The pants you rolled up for him by the barn?"

"Pants? Oh, yes, they were too long after all. So what of it?"

The glaringly smooth wall of a lie told in good faith, a lie that she did not feel to be a lie. But how could I demand truth from her? This creature, sitting next to me, small, frail, ill-defined, who was not yet a woman but merely a prelude to a woman, this transience that existed solely to cease being what it is now, that was killing itself.

"Karol is in love with you!"

"Him? He's not in love with me, or with anybody else. . . . All he wants is, well . . . to go to bed with somebody . . ." and here she said something that pleased her, she expressed it as follows: "After all, he's just a kid, and besides, you know . . . well, better not talk about that!" This was of course an allusion to Karol's uncertain past, but in spite of everything, I thought I was also catching a friendly tone toward him—as if there was the shadow of a "limited" friendliness hiding here, somewhat collegial, she did not say it with disgust, no, but rather said it as if it pleased her to some degree . . . and even intimately in some way. . . . It seemed that as Vaclav's fiancée she was judging Karol severely, but also, at the same time, she was associating herself with his tumultuous fate, common to all born under the sign of war. I latched onto this right away, and I too struck the chord of intimacy, I said, nonchalantly and like a colleague, that after all, she must have slept with more than one man, surely she's no saint, so she could go to bed with him too, and why not? She accepted it easily, more easily than I expected and even with a certain eagerness, with a strange obedience. She promptly agreed with me that "she could of course" and especially since it had already happened with someone from the Underground Army who stayed overnight at the house, last year. "Don't tell my parents, of course." But why was this young girl introducing me so easily into her little affairs? And right after her betrothal to Vaclav? I asked whether her parents suspected anything (with regard to the one from the UA), to which she replied: "They suspect it, since they caught us at it. But *actually* they don't suspect it. . . ."

"Actually"—a brilliant word. With its help one can say anything. A brilliantly obfuscating word. We were now descending down the road toward Brzustowa, among linden trees—shadow is bathed in sunlight, the horses slow down, the harness moves forward on their necks, the sand creaks under the wheels.

"Good! Well, then! Why not? If with that one from the UA, why not with this one?"

"No."

The ease with which women say "no." This talent for refusal. This "no," always at the ready—and when they find it within them, they're merciless. Yet . . . could she be in love with Vaclav? Is this where the restraint came from? I said something to this effect: it would be a blow for Vaclav if he found out about her "past"—he who worships her and is so religious, so principled. I expressed the hope that she would not tell him, yes, better to spare him this . . . spare the one who believes in their total spiritual understanding . . . She interrupted me, offended. "And what do you think? That I have no morality?"

"He has a Catholic morality."

"Me too. It's the truth, I am a Catholic."

"What do you mean? Do you take the sacraments?"

"Of course!"

"Do you believe in God? Literally, as a true Catholic?"

"If I didn't believe, I wouldn't be going to confession and Holy Communion. And don't think anything to the contrary! My future husband's principles suit me just fine. And his mother is almost a mother to me. You'll see, what a woman! It's an honor for me to become part of such a family." And after a moment's silence she added, hitting the horses with the reins: "At least when I marry him I won't be screwing around."

Sand. Road. We're going uphill.

The vulgarity of her last words—what was that for? "I won't be screwing around." She could have put it more subtly. But the undertone of her sentence was double-edged. . . . It contained a desire for purity, dignity—and at the same time it was unworthy of her, degrading in its actual wording . . . and exciting me anew . . . exciting me . . . because it again brought her closer to Karol. And once more, as with Karol earlier, a fleeting discouragement came upon me—that we can't find out anything from them because everything they say, or think, or feel, is only a game of excitement, a constant teasing, a kindling of a narcissistic savoring of themselves—and that they are the first to fall prey to their own seductions. This young girl? This young girl who was nothing but a captivating force, an attraction, a greatly appealing element, unceasing, lithe, soft, absorbent coquetry—and she was like this as she sat next to me, in her little coat, with her little hands that were too small. "When I marry him I won't screw around." This sounded severe, taking herself in hand—for Vaclav, because of Vaclav—but it was also an intimate, and oh how seductive, admission of her own weakness. She was therefore exciting even in her virtue. . . and in the distance ahead of us was the carriage, mounting a hill, and on the coach box next to the coachman was Karol . . . Karol . . . Karol . . . On the coach box. On the hill. In the distance. I don't know whether it was the fact that he appeared "in the distance"—or that he appeared "on the hill"—yet in this configuration, in this "rendering" of Karol, in this appearance of his, there was something infuriating me, and, furious, pointing my finger at him, I said:

"But you like to crush earthworms with him!"

"Why are you stuck on that earthworm? He stepped on it, so I stepped on it."

"You both knew quite well the worm was suffering!"

"What do you mean?"

Again nothing was revealed. She sat next to me. For a moment the thought came to me to let go—to back out. . . . My situation, my bathing in their eroticism—oh, it was impossible! I should get busy with something else as soon as possible, something more appropriate—busy with more serious matters! Would it be so difficult to return to normal, to the truly familiar state in which other things seem interesting and important, while such antics with young people become worthy of nothing but disdain? But what if one gets excited, loves one's excitement, excites oneself with it, and everything else is no longer alive! Once more pointing to Karol with my shaming finger, I emphatically declared, my intent being to press her to the wall, to wrest an admission from her:

"You're not just for yourself. You're for someone else. And in this case you're for him. You belong to him!"

"Me? To him? What put that into your head?"

She laughed. This laughter of theirs, constant, unceasing—hers and his—obfuscating everything! What misery.

She was pushing him away . . . by laughing. . . . She was pushing him away with laughter. This laughter of hers was short, it soon ceased, it was merely a hint of laughter—but in this brief moment I saw his laughter through her laughter. The same laughing mouths with teeth inside them. This was "cute" . . . unfortunately, unfortunately, this was "cute." They were both "cute." That's why she didn't want it!

VII

Ruda. We spilled out of the two vehicles in front of the porch. Vaclav appeared and ran to greet his future wife at the threshold of his home—welcoming us with an engaging, composed courtesy. In the hall we kissed the hand of the elderly lady's, petite and wizened, she gave off the aroma of herbs and medicaments—and she diligently and carefully pressed our fingers. The house was full of people, yesterday the hosts' family had unexpectedly arrived from the vicinity of Lvov, they were put up on the second floor, there were beds in the living room, the servant girl ran around busily, children were playing on the floor among bundles and suitcases. This being so, we volunteered to go back to Poworna for the night—but Madame Amelia wouldn't agree, and she pleaded "Don't do this to me," surely we would all fit in somehow. Other reasons also argued for a quick return home, Vaclav revealed to us, the men, that two people from the Underground Army had arrived asking to be put up for the night, and, from their brief intimations, it seemed that some action was being planned in this area. All this created a state of anxiety—but we sat in the armchairs in the somewhat darkened, many-windowed living room and began talking, while Madame Amelia graciously addressed Fryderyk and me, asking about our ups and downs and our adventures. Her head, old beyond her age and desiccated, was rising above her neck like a star, she was undoubtedly someone exceptional, and in general the atmosphere of this place turned out to be inordinately powerful, the paeans in her honor had not been exaggerated, no, we were dealing not with an upright, rural patron of merely provincial dimension but with someone whose presence imposed itself with a mighty power. It's hard to describe the basis for it. A respect for the human being, similar to Vaclav's, but perhaps even deeper. Politeness, derived from truly refined values. Gentleness, full of deep feeling, inspired, yet marked by immense simplicity. And a strange integrity. However, deep down it was extraordinarily clear-cut, here reigned a higher reason, absolute, cutting through any doubts, and for us, for me and probably for Fryderyk, this house, with such a well-defined morality, suddenly became a wonderful rest, an oasis. Because a metaphysical, that is, beyond-the-body, principle reigned here, in brief, there reigned here the Catholic God, liberated from the body and far too dignified to chase after Henia and Karol. It was as if the hand of a wise mother had given us a spanking and we were called to order, while everything returned to its proper dimension. Henia with Karol, Henia plus Karol, became what they were, ordinary youths—while Henia with Vaclav acquired a meaning, but only because of love and marriage. While we, the elders, regained the raison d'être of our seniority, we suddenly became set in it so firmly that it was impossible to conceive of any threat from the other thing, from down below. In a word, there was a repeat of that "sobering up" that Vaclav had brought for us to Poworna, but to a greater degree. The crushing pressure on our chest of the young knees was no more.

Fryderyk came to life. Released from their accursed knees, their crushing legs, he seemed to regain a belief in himself—he breathed with relief—all at once he was dazzling with his full brightness. The things he said were by no means brilliant, merely ordinary, and he said them only to keep the conversation going—yet every trifle, loaded with his personality, his experience, his consciousness, gained importance. The simplest word, "window" for example, or "bread," or "thank you," acquired a totally different flavor on those lips that knew so well "what they were saying." He said, "One likes small pleasures," and this too became important, even though its importance was discretely masked. His particular modus became highly palpable, his way of being as the fruit of his development and life experiences—this is what suddenly became most concretely present—and actually, if one has as much value as one attaches to oneself, then in this case we were dealing with a giant, with a colossus, because it was hard not to realize what an unparalleled phenomenon he sensed himself to be—unparalleled not on the scale of social values, but as a being, as an existence. And so Vaclav and his mother received this solitary greatness of his with open arms, as if giving him their respect was their greatest pleasure. Even Henia, surely the most important person in this house, was displaced to the background, and everything began to revolve around Fryderyk.

"Let us go," Amelia said, "I'll show you the view of the river from the terrace before lunch is served."

She was so absorbed by him that she turned only to him, forgetting Henia, forgetting us. . . . We went out with them onto the terrace, from which, in lively slopes, the land slipped down into the smoothness of the watery ribbon, hardly visible and as if inanimate. This was not ugly. Yet Fryderyk inadvertently said:

"A barrel."

He was thrown off balance . . . because, instead of admiring the landscape he had noticed something as inferior as a barrel, something commonplace, abandoned under a tree, to one side. He didn't know how he chanced upon it, and he didn't know how to extricate himself from it. While Madame Amelia repeated:

"A barrel."

She seconded him softly yet quite perceptively, sort of acquiescing and agreeing with him in some eager and instant accord—as if she were no stranger to such accidental initiations into accidental matters, forming an unexpected attachment to any object that, on the strength of this attachment, becomes the most important thing. . . . Oh, those two had a lot in common! In addition to ourselves, the refugee family sat to lunch with their children—so many people at the table, this crowd, and children running around, and the improvised eating arrangement, it wasn't good for our mood . . . the lunch was tiresome. And they kept mulling over "the situation," in general, in connection with the German retreat, as much as the local one, while I was getting lost in their discourse in their native country lingo, different from the Warsaw one. I only understood the half of it, but I didn't ask any questions, I didn't want to ask about anything, I knew it was not worth bothering about, and besides, it wouldn't be advisable to do so, why bother, I would know soon enough, in the midst of this palaver I went on drinking, and I knew well enough that, while she was tirelessly running everything from the heights of her wizened little head, Madame Amelia was constantly addressing herself to Fryderyk with a singular alertness, with an exceptional concentration, indeed, with tension—she seemed to be in love with him. . . . Love? It was the magic, rather, of his seemingly inexhaustible awareness, the same that I too had experienced so many times. He was so deeply, so irrevocably aware! And Amelia, undoubtedly sharpened by repeated meditation and repeated effort, immediately sniffed who she was dealing with. Someone intensely focused, someone who would not allow anything to pull him away from the ultimate—no matter what kind of person she happened to be—someone serious to the farthest limits, in relation to whom all the others were merely children. Having discovered Fryderyk, she passionately wished to know how this guest would behave toward her—whether he would accept her or whether he would reject her, together with the truth that she had fostered within herself.

She guessed that he was a nonbeliever—one sensed this from her particular circumspection, from the distance she kept. She knew that this precipice existed between them, yet in spite of it, it was from him that she expected recognition and affirmation. The others, the people whom she had encountered thus far, were believers, but their beliefs were not deep enough—while this man, a nonbeliever, was boundlessly deep, and he therefore could not disregard her depth, he was "ultimate," so he had to grasp her ultimate limits as well—he "knew," after all, he "understood," he "felt." Amelia was bent on measuring her own ultimate limits against his ultimate limits, I think that she was like a provincial artist who wants to show his work to a connoisseur for the first time—but this work was herself, it was her life, for which she demanded recognition. But, as I said before, she was unable to express it, she probably would not have been able to do so even if atheism were not the obstacle. Nevertheless the presence of someone else's depth roused all of her inner depths, and she tried to convey to him, at least with her intensity and readiness, how anxious she was to have him on her side and what she expected from him.

As to Fryderyk, he behaved, as usual, beyond reproach and with the greatest tact. His baseness, however, just as when he was hoeing and admitting defeat, began to slowly show its presence under her influence. It was the baseness of impotence. The whole thing was reminiscent of copulation, a spiritual one of course. Amelia demanded that he acknowledge her faith, if not her God, yet this man was incapable of such an act, condemned as he was to the eternal terror of what is, in its coldness, warmed by nothing—he was as he was—he just watched Amelia, acknowledging that she was as she was. It was precisely this that, in the rays of her warmth, became corpselike, helpless. And his atheism grew under the influence of her theism, they soon became entangled in this disastrous contradiction. And his corporeality also grew under the influence of her spirituality, and his hand, for instance, became very, very, very much a hand (which, I don't know why, reminded me of that earthworm). I also caught the gaze with which he was disrobing Amelia, like a Don Juan disrobing a little girl, a gaze that clearly wondered how she would look naked—not because of some erotic impulse, of course, but just to know better whom one was conversing with. She curled up under his gaze and suddenly became silent—she understood that for him she was merely what she was for him, nothing more.

This took place on the terrace, after lunch. She rose from an armchair and turned to him:

"Please give me your arm. We'll walk a bit."

She leaned on his arm. Perhaps in this way, by touching physically, she wanted to encourage familiarity and to overcome his corporeality! The two of them walked, close, side by side, like a couple of lovers, the six of us following behind, like a procession—this really looked like a romance, wasn't it the same way that we had recently accompanied Henia and Vaclav?

A romance, yet a tragic one. I think that Amelia felt an unpleasant tremor when she caught his disrobing gaze—because no one had ever approached her like this, because it was nothing but respect and love that she had experienced from those surrounding her since her earliest years. So what did he know and what kind of knowledge was this—to treat her like this? She was absolutely sure that the solidity of her spiritual effort which had earned her people's goodwill could not be subject to doubt, hence she was actually not afraid for herself, she was afraid for the world—because here her view of the world was countered by another view, no less serious, also dictated by something like a retreat to ultimate positions. . . .

These two serious presences trod beside one another, arm in arm, over the vast meadow, while the sun was sinking and assuming larger proportions, reddening, and long shadows were springing up from us. Henia walked with Vaclav. Hipolit with Maria. I on the side. And Karol. The couple ahead of us, deep in their dialogue. But the dialogue did not express anything. They talked about . . . Venice.

At one moment she stopped.

"Please look around. How beautiful it is!"

He replied:

"Yes, no doubt about it. Very beautiful."

It was said to second her.

She trembled with sudden impatience. His response had no substance—it was merely to avoid a proper response—even though carefully delivered and with feeling—but with the feeling of an actor. While she was demanding a genuine admiration of the evening, this being God's creation, and she wanted him to adore the Creator at least in his work. Her purity was intrinsic to this desire.

"But please really look, be truthful. Isn't this very beautiful?"

This time, called to order, he tried to focus, it was obvious he made an effort and actually spoke as sincerely as he could, and even with some emotion.

"Yes indeed, beautiful to be sure, yes, wonderful!"

She couldn't fault this. It was apparent that he was making an effort to satisfy her. Except for his disastrous characteristic: that in saying something it seemed that he was saying it in order not to say something else. . . . But what? Amelia decided to show her cards and, not moving from where she stood, she stated:

"You are an atheist."

Before he expressed his opinion on such a delicate matter he cast his gaze right and left, as if checking up on the world. He said . . . because he had to, because he had nothing else to say, because his response had already been determined by her question:

"I am an atheist."

But again he said this in order not to say *something else!* One could sense it! She fell silent, as if her chance for polemics had been cut short. If he were truly a nonbeliever, she could have fought with him, then she would have demonstrated the most profound "extremity" of her own reasoning, ha, she would have been fighting with her equal. But for him, words served only to conceal . . . something else. But what? What? If he was neither a believer nor a nonbeliever, what was he? A swath of something undefined was opening up, of a strange "otherness" where she was lost, bewildered, knocked out of the game.

She turned back to the house, and we all followed her, casting kilometer-long shadows that, spreading over the meadow, were reaching distant places, unfamiliar to us, somewhere at the far end of a stubble field. A wonderful evening. She was—I'd swear—truly frightened. She walked, no longer paying attention to Fryderyk, who was nonetheless accompanying her genially—like a little dog. Knocked out of the game . . . she was like someone whose weapon had been knocked from her hand. No one was attacking her faith—she didn't need to defend it—God was becoming superfluous in the face of an atheism that was only a screen—and she felt alone, without God, thrown on her own resources in relation to this other existence, based on an unknown principle that was escaping her. And the fact . . . that it was escaping her—was discrediting her. It showed that a Catholic spirit might encounter, on a perfectly even road, something unknown to him, something he had not foreseen, something beyond his control. She was suddenly seized by someone in a manner unfamiliar to her—and she became something incomprehensible to herself through Fryderyk!

That evening, on this meadow, our walk elongated itself, like a snake. Somewhat behind us, diagonally across and to the left, walked Henia with Vaclav, both very courteous, civilized, settled in their own families, he—his mother's son, she—her parents' daughter, and the attorney's body didn't feel ill at ease with a sixteen-year-old, having the sum of two mothers and a father by his side. While Karol walked by himself, to one side, his hands in his pockets, he was bored, or perhaps he wasn't even bored, he was merely putting his feet on the grass, left, then right, then left, then right, then left, then right, then left, in this spacious green-as-a-meadow loafing of his, while the sinking, setting sun was warming us and a breeze was cooling us—and so he was setting his feet down, setting them here and there, sometimes he slowed down, sometimes he went faster, until he finally caught up with Fryderyk (who walked with Madame Amelia). For a while they walked side by side. Karol said:

"You could give me your old jacket."

"What for?

"I need one. For business."

"So what if you need it?"

"I need it!" Karol repeated insolently, laughing.

"Then buy one yourself," Fryderyk replied.

"I don't have any dough."

"I don't have any either."

"Just give me your jacket!"

Madame Amelia picked up the pace—so did Fryderyk—and Karol did too.

"Just give me your jacket!"

"Just give him your jacket!"

This was Henia. She joined them. Her fiancé stayed a bit behind. She was walking with Karol, her voice, her movements were like his.

"Just give him your jacket!"

"Just give me your jacket!"

Fryderyk stood still, lifted his arms jokingly: "Leave me alone, children!" Amelia began walking away faster and faster, not looking back at them, she therefore looked like someone who is pursued. Really—why didn't she turn her head even once? This mistake turned her into someone running from juvenile scamps (while her son remained in the background). The question was whom was she running from: from them or from him, Fryderyk? Or from him with them? It didn't seem likely that she had sniffed anything of the little affairs happening among those juveniles, no, she didn't have a nose for it, they were too much her inferiors—because Henia meant something to her only with Vaclav, as his future wife, while Henia with Karol, they were just children, young people. So if she were running away it was from Fryderyk, from the familiarity that Karol was allowing himself with him—incomprehensible to her—the familiarity that was suddenly created here, next to her, striking a blow at her . . .

because this man, overtaken by the boy, was thereby destroying and losing the seriousness that he had created within himself and in relation to her. . . . And this familiarity had been reinforced by her son's fiancée! Amelia's flight was an admission that she had noticed it, had taken it in!

When she walked away, those two stopped pressing Fryderyk for his jacket. Because she had walked away? Or because their jocularity had run its course? I needn't add that Fryderyk, though shaken by this youthful onslaught and looking like someone who had barely escaped a gang on the outskirts of town in the middle of the night, took the utmost precautions that some "wolf from the woods," the wolf that he did not know, that he always feared, would not be called forth. Quickly joining Hipolit and Maria, he began to "talk away" these improprieties, he even called to Vaclav to engage him as well in this simple, relaxing conversation. And for the remainder of the evening he was quiet as a mouse, didn't even look at them, at Henia with Karol, at Karol with Henia, his aim was to calm and defuse the situation. He was undoubtedly afraid of stirring up the depths to which Amelia allowed herself to go with regard to him. He was afraid of it, especially in a combination with that shallow, youthful frivolity, that recklessness, he sensed that the two dimensions could not coexist, so he was afraid of something blowing apart and irrupting into . . . what? What? Yes, yes, he was afraid of the exploding mixture, of the A (i.e., "Amelia") multiplied by (H + K). So, swallowing his pride, tail between his legs, he went mum, shush! At supper (it took place in the family circle, because the refugees from Lvov were served their food upstairs) he even went as far as to raise a toast in honor of the betrothed, wishing them all the best with his whole heart. It would be hard to match this propriety. Unfortunately, here too the mechanism by means of which Fryderyk was prone to sink deeper, even as he tried to back out, made itself known—but in this case it happened in a particularly violent, even dramatic way. His sudden rising to his feet and the emergence of his person among us who were seated created unwelcome panic, and Madame Maria was unable to hold back a nervous "oh"—because it wasn't obvious what he was going to say, what he would say. Yet his initial sentences turned out to be soothing, they were conventional, spiked with humor—while waving his napkin, he gave thanks for making his bachelorhood pleasant with such a moving betrothal, and, with a few rounded turns of phrase he described the betrothed as a nice couple . . . but as his speech progressed, behind his words something was mounting that he was not saying, oh, constantly the same story! . . . In the end, and to the horror of the speaker himself, it became clear that his speech merely served to turn our attention away from his real speech that was taking place in silence, beyond words, and expressing what words did not encompass. Cutting through the courteous platitudes, his actual being gained voice, nothing could erase the face, the eyes expressing some relentless fact—and, sensing that he was becoming frightful and thus dangerous to himself as well, he stood on his head to be nice, he conducted his conciliatory rhetoric in an arch-moral spirit, arch-Catholic, about "family as the unit of society" and about "venerable traditions." At the same time, however, he was hitting Amelia and everyone else in the face with his face that was deprived of illusions and inescapably present. The power of his "speech" was stupendous indeed. The most shattering oration I ever happened to hear. And one could see that the power, so parenthetic, so incidental, carried the speaker away like a horse!

He finished with wishes for happiness. He said something like this:

"Ladies and gentlemen, they deserve happiness, so they will be happy."

Which meant:

"I'm talking just to talk."

Madame Amelia hurriedly said:

"We are very, very grateful!"

Clinking our glasses erased the horror, and Amelia, exceedingly gracious, concentrated on her duties as the lady of the house: More meat, anyone? Perhaps vodka? . . . Everyone started talking, just to hear his own voice, and in this chatter we all felt better. Cheesecake was served. Toward the end of supper Madame Amelia rose and went to the pantry, while we, warmed by the vodka, joked around, telling the young lady what and how one had eaten on similar occasions before the war, and what delicacies she was missing. Karol laughed good-naturedly and sincerely, handing in his empty glass. I noticed that Amelia, who had returned from the pantry, sat on her chair in a strange way—first she stood next to it, then, after a moment and as if on command, she sat down—I had no time to think about it as she fell to the floor from the chair. Everyone jumped to his feet. We saw a red stain on the floor. A woman's scream sounded from the kitchen, then a shot rang outside the windows, and someone, probably Hipolit, threw a jacket over the lamp. Darkness and a shot again. Abrupt closing of doors, Amelia was carried to the couch, feverish activity in the darkness. The jacket on the lamp began to smolder, they trampled it, somehow things immediately quieted down, everyone was listening intently, while Vaclav pressed a shotgun into my hand and pushed me to the window in the adjoining room: "Be careful!" I saw a quiet night in the garden, moonlit, while a partially dried-up leaf, on a branch that looked into the window, twirled every now and then with its little silver belly. I was clutching the weapon and watching to see if anyone was emerging from there, from the spot where the dampness of the twisted tree trunks began. But only a sparrow moved in the thicket. Finally a door banged, someone spoke loudly, people were saying something again, and I realized that the panic had passed.

Madame Maria appeared next to me. "Do you know anything about medicine? Come. She's dying. She was stabbed with a knife. . . . Do you know anything about medicine?"

Amelia was lying on the couch, her head on a pillow, the room was full of people—the refugee family, the servants. . . . I was struck by the immobility of these people, impotence wafted from them . . . the same impotence that was often apparent in Fryderyk. . . . They stood back from her and left her alone so she could deal with her dying. They were merely assisting. Her profile stood out immobile, like a rocky promontory, and near by were Vaclav, Fryderyk, Hipolit—standing . . . Will she take long to die? On the floor a bowl of cotton wool and blood. But Amelia's body was not the only body lying in this room, there, on the floor, in a corner, lay another . . . and I didn't know what that was, where it had come from, I couldn't tell who was lying there, and at the same time I felt there was something erotic . . . that something erotic had come straggling in here . . . Karol? Where was Karol? Leaning with his hand on a chair he was standing, like everyone else, while Henia was kneeling, her hands on an armchair. And everyone was leaning toward Amelia so I couldn't get a closer look at the other body, supernumerary and unexpected. No one stirred. But everyone watched anxiously, with questioning looks. How will she die—because one would have expected from her a death more dignified than an ordinary death, and this is what her son, and the Hipolits, and Henia were expecting of her, and even Fryderyk, who wasn't taking his eyes off her. This was paradoxical, because they were demanding action from a person who was unable to move, frozen in powerlessness, and yet she was the only one here called upon to act. She knew it. Suddenly Madame Hipolit ran out and returned with a crucifix, this was like a call to action addressed to the dying woman, and the burden of waiting fell from our hearts—now we knew that something would soon begin. Madame Maria, cross in hand, stood next to the couch.

Then something happened that was so outrageous that in spite of all its nicety it looked like a blow. . . . The dying woman, barely touching the cross with her gaze, turned her eyes sideways toward Fryderyk and she united with him with her gaze—this was unbelievable, no one would have thought of the possibility of her avoiding the cross that now, in Madame Maria's hands, became superfluous—and this very avoidance added to Amelia's gaze, now fixed on Fryderyk, so much weight. Poor Fryderyk froze, caught by the dying and therefore dangerous gaze, and, pale, he stood almost at attention—they were looking at each other. Madame Maria continued to hold the cross, but minutes passed and it remained idle—the doleful, unemployed crucifix. Could it be that for this saint, in her hour of death, Fryderyk had become more important than Christ? So was she really in love with him? Yet this was not love, this had to do with something even more personal, this woman saw in him her judge—she could not accept the fact that she would die without having brought him around to herself, without having proved that she was no less "ultimate" than he, equally fundamental, a phenomenon that was essential, no less important. That's how much she relied upon his opinion. However, the fact that she was turning not to

Christ for recognition and for validation of her existence but to him, to a mortal, albeit endowed with uncommon consciousness, was an astounding heresy on her part, a repudiation of the absolute for the sake of life, an admission that not God but man is to be man's judge. Perhaps I didn't understand it so clearly at the time, nonetheless, shivers went through me at this uniting of her gaze with a human being, while God, in Maria's hands, remained unnoticed.

Her dying, which actually did not progress at all, became, under the pressure of our concentration and our waiting, more tense from moment to moment—we were the ones loading it with our tension. And I knew Fryderyk well enough to worry that, while facing human death, something so special, he would no longer be able to bear it and would commit some impropriety. . . . But he stood, as if at attention, as if in church, and the only thing one could reproach him for was that every so often his eyes would abandon Amelia against his will to reach into the back of the room where the other body lay, mysterious to me, that I actually could not see well from my spot, but Fryderyk's progressively more frequent forays with his eyes made me finally decide to go and look . . . and I approached that corner. Oh, what terror, what agitation I felt when I saw (a boy) whose leanness was a duplication of (Karol's) leanness, he lay there and was alive, and, what's more, he was the embodiment of blond charm with dark, huge eyes, and his darkness and swarthiness were drowning in the wildness of his hands and bare legs curled on the floor!

A wild, predatory, blond youth, barefoot, from the village, yet breathing forth beauty—a gorgeous, grimy little god who was here on the floor acting out his surly seductions. This body? This body? What did this body mean here? Why was he lying here? And so . . . this was a reiteration of Karol but in a lower register . . . and suddenly youth was mounting in the room not only numerically (because two is one thing, three is another), but in its very quality as well, it became something different, wilder and lower. And straight away, as if in repercussion, Karol's body came to life, more intense and powerful, while Henia, though pious and kneeling, came tumbling down with all her whiteness into the realm of sinful and secret understanding with these two. At the same time Amelia's throes of death became tainted, somehow suspect—what was her connection with this young, rustic, good-looking fellow, why did this (boy) come straggling up to her in her dying hour? I realized that this death was happening in ambiguous circumstances, much more ambiguous than they seemed on the surface. . . .

Fryderyk, forgetting himself, put his hand in his pocket, then quickly took it out, then dropped his hands by his side.

Vaclav was kneeling.

Madame Maria was tirelessly holding the cross because there was nothing else she could do—setting it aside would have been out of the question.

Amelia's finger quivered and lifted and began to beckon . . . it beckoned and beckoned . . . toward Fryderyk, who approached her slowly and cautiously. She also beckoned toward his head until he stooped over her, and then she said astonishingly loudly:

"Please don't leave. You will see. I want you to see. Everything. To the end."

Fryderyk bowed and stepped back.

Only then did she fix her eyes on the cross and, I imagine, prayed, if one were to judge by the quivering that from time to time appeared on her lips—and in the end it was as it should be, the cross, her prayer, our attention—and this lasted an exceedingly long time, and the passage of time was the only measure of the fervor of these unending prayers that could not tear themselves from the cross. And this immobile and almost dead yet vibrating concentration, mounting with time, was sanctifying her, in the meantime Vaclav, the Hipolits, Henia, the servants, attended her on bended knee. Fryderyk also knelt down. But in vain. Because in spite of everything, and even though she was so lost in the cross, her demand that he see it retained its power. Why did she need this? To convert him with her last dying effort? To show him how one dies the Catholic way? Whatever it was that she wanted it was Fryderyk, not Christ, who was her final court of appeal, even if she were praying to Christ, it was for Fryderyk, and it made no difference that he fell to his knees, it was he, not Christ, who became the highest judge and God, because the death throes were taking place for him. What a baffling situation—I wasn't surprised that he hid his face in his hands. All the more since, as the minutes were passing, we knew that with each minute her life was ebbing away—yet she was prolonging her prayer just so that it would stretch like a violin string, to the very limit. And again her finger appeared and began to beckon, this time toward her son. Vaclav approached, his arm around Henia. The finger directed itself straight at them, and Amelia said with haste:

"Swear to me immediately, now . . . Love and fidelity. Quick."

They lowered their heads to her hands, Henia began to cry. But the finger rose again and beckoned, now in the other direction—to the corner, where in the corner lay . . . There was a commotion. He was lifted—and I saw that he was wounded, in the thigh I think—they carried him to her. She moved her lips, and I thought that I would finally find out what this was, why he was here with her, this (young one), also bleeding, what was between them. . . . But suddenly she gasped, once, twice, and went pale. Madame Maria raised the cross. Madame Amelia fixed her eyes on Fryderyk and died.

Part II

VIII

Fryderyk rose from his knees and stepped into the center of the room: "Pay her your respects!" he exclaimed. "Pay homage!" He took the roses from a vase and threw them toward the couch, then he reached out his hand to Vaclav. "A soul worthy of the heavenly choir! While for us there is nothing left but to bow our heads!" These words would have been theatrical on any of our lips, not to mention his gestures, but he pierced us with them imperiously, like a king to whom pathos is permitted—who lays down a different kind of naturalness, above the ordinary. A ruling king, master of ceremonies! Vaclav, swept away by the sovereignty of this pathos, rose from his knees and ardently clasped his hand. It seemed that Fryderyk aimed his intervention at erasing all the strange improprieties that had cast a shadow over the demise, to return it to its full splendor. He moved a few steps to the left, then to the right—this was a kind of agitation in our midst—and he approached the lying (boy). "Rise to your knees!" he commanded. "To your knees!" This command was, on the one hand, the natural extension of the previous command, but, on the other hand, it created an awkwardness, because it was directed at the wounded man who was unable to rise, and the awkwardness increased when Vaclav, Hipolit, and Karol, terrorized by Fryderyk's authority, rushed to raise (the boy) to the commanded position. Yes, this was going too far! As Karol's hands took him under the arms, Fryderyk, thrown off track, fell silent, and his lights went out.

I was bewildered, exhausted . . . so much was happening . . . but I had already taken his measure . . . and so I knew that he had once more taken up his game with us and with himself. . . . From the tension, created by the corpse, some action of his was evolving, leading to a goal rooted in his imagination. It had all been intentional, though the intention was perhaps not yet tangible even to himself, perhaps one should say that he knew only the preamble to the intention—but I would have been surprised if what he had in mind was homage to Amelia, no, this had to do with bringing to us the man who was lying, in all his drastic and humiliating sense, with "pulling him out," enhancing him and "binding him" with Henia and Karol. What connection, however, could there be between them? This golden wildness surely fit in with our couple, if only because it was also a sixteen-year-old wildness, but beyond that I didn't see any connection, and I think that Fryderyk did not see one either—he acted in the dark, prompted by a sense, as unclear as my own, that he, the lying man, is enhancing their power—turning them into demons. . . . And thus Fryderyk was paving the lying man's way to them.

Not until the following day (filled with preparations for the funeral) did I find out in some detail about the course of these disastrous events—which were extremely complex, bizarre, eerie. Reconstruction of the facts was not easy, there were many distressing gaps—especially since the only witnesses, this Józek, Józek Skuziak, and the old servant woman, Waleria, were lost in the chaos inside their incompetent and uneducated heads. Everything indicated that Madame Amelia, having gone into the pantry, heard murmurs on the stairs leading to the kitchen and bumped into this Józek, who had slipped into the house to filch something. On hearing her steps, he threw himself into the first door he saw and ran into the small servant's room, awakening Waleria from a deep sleep, whereupon she lit a match. The further course of events unfolded primarily from her garbled account. "When I lit a match, and when I saw that someone was standin', I froze so I couldn't even move, and the match was burnin' down in my fingers, my whole finger got burned. And m' ladyship is standin' there across from him, by the door, and she ain't movin' either. The match went out on me. I couldn't see nothin', the window shade was down, I'm lyin' there, lookin', don't see nothin', it's dark, wish at least the floor would creak, but nothin', nothin', like nobody's there, I'm lyin', just givin' m'self to God, still nothin', it's quiet, so I look at the floor because that's where the last of the flame of the match is glowin' but lightin' up nothin', it burns out, nothin', wish somebody would breathe or somethin', but nothin'. All of a sudden . . ." (her account halted as if it came upon logs thrown crosswise) . . . "all of a sudden . . . somethin's odd . . . it's m' ladyship that flings herself! On top o' him! . . . Under his feet like . . . she must have thrown herself . . . So they fell down! . . . I don't know nothin', may God's hand spare us, would at least one o' them get to swearin', but nothin', nothin', they just tussled on the floor like, I wanted to help 'em, but no way, I got faint, I hear a knife go deep into meat, once, twice, I hear agin knife into meat, then the two of them took to the door an' that's that! So I passed out totally! I passed out!"

Vaclav heatedly commented "That's impossible!" to her account. "It couldn't have happened like that! I don't believe mother would have . . . behaved that way! The hag must have mixed things up, muddled them up in her stupidity. Oh, I'd rather listen to a hen cackling, I'd rather," he exclaimed, "a hen cackling!"

He was moving his hand across his brow.

But Skuziak's deposition agreed with what Waleria was saying: her ladyship fell and "knocked him down," because she fell "at his feet." With a knife. And he showed not only his slashed side and thigh, but also clear marks of bites on his neck and hands. "She was bitin'," he said. "I snatched the knife from her, so then she got stuck on the knife, so I jumped away and took off, but the farm manager came after me shootin', my leg went soft, so I sat down. . . . They caught me."

Well, the fact that Amelia "got stuck" on the knife no one believed. "Lies," Fryderyk said. "As to the bites, my God, fighting for one's life, in a convulsive fight with an armed thug (because he was the one with the knife, not she) . . . well, nerves . . . One can't be surprised. It's an instinct, you know, a self-preservation instinct. . . ." That's what he was saying. Nonetheless it was all strange, to say the least . . . and shocking . . . Madame Amelia biting someone . . . And as far as the knife was concerned, the matter wasn't clear because, as it turned out, it was Waleria's knife, a long, sharp kitchen knife that she used for cutting bread. So this knife lay on a small table beside her bed, exactly where Amelia had stood. Which would indicate that she, Amelia, feeling the knife in the dark with her fingers, threw herself with it onto . . .

Amelia's murderer was barefoot, had dark feet, and he sparkled with two rather ordinary colors—the gold of his curly hair falling over the black of his eyes imbued with glumness, like those of forest puddles. These colors were especially intensified by the elegant, clear shine of his teeth, whose whiteness connected him with . . .

Then what? Then how? Then it would seem that Madame Amelia, finding herself in the dark little room with this (boy) and in the claws of intensifying anticipation, broke down and . . . and . . . She felt for the knife with her fingers. And having felt it, she went wild. She threw herself onto him to kill, and when they both fell, she bit him like a madwoman wherever she could. She? With her sanctity? At her age? She, such an exemplar, with her moral code? Wasn't this rather a fantasy born in the cook's and the farmhand's dull-witted pates, a wild tale to their measure, created by a transformation of what had played out in the dark, which was actually intangible? The darkness of the little room was doubled by the darkness of their imagination—and Vaclav, besieged by these darknesses that were knocking him off his feet, didn't know what to do, this was for him, more than the knife, what was killing his mother, poisoning her for him and disfiguring her—he didn't know how to rescue her for himself from this fury inscribed on the sixteen-year-old body with her teeth, with the knife with which she cut him. Such death tore her life into shreds for him. Fryderyk tried, as much as he could, to support him in spirit. "One can't rely on their testimony," he said. "First of all, they didn't see anything because it was dark. Second, it's totally unlike your mother, it doesn't fit—there is only one thing we can say, and this we can say with absolute certainty, that it couldn't have happened the way they're describing it, it must have happened some other way, in that darkness as inaccessible to them as it is to us . . . it's the truth, no doubt about it . . . though of course, if in the darkness, then . . ." ("Then what? Then what?" Vaclav kept asking, sensing that Fryderyk faltered.) "Then . . . well . . . well, the darkness, mind you . . . darkness is something . . . that throws one off from . . . One must remember that man lives in the world. In the dark the world disappears. There is nothing around, you know, one is just with oneself. Of course you know that. We are naturally accustomed to the fact that each time we turn off a lamp, it becomes dark, this doesn't however rule out the fact that in certain instances darkness can blind us through and through, you understand . . . and yet Madame Amelia would have, even in this darkness, remained Madame Amelia, isn't that so? Though in this case the darkness held something within it . . . ("What?" Vaclav asked. "Tell me!") "Nothing, nothing, it's idiotic, it's nonsense . . . ("What is?") "Oh nothing, yet . . . this young fellow, from the village, maybe an illiterate . . ." ("So what if he's an illiterate?") "Nothing, nothing, I just want to say that in this case the darkness held youth within itself . . . it held a barefooted young fellow . . . and it's easier to commit something like this on someone young than on someone . . . I mean, if it were someone more grown-up, then . . ." ("Then what?!) I mean to say that it's easier with a young person, yes, easier—in the dark—it's easier to commit something like this against a young one rather than against an old one, and . . .

"Oh, stop pumping me, Vaclav!" he suddenly exclaimed, truly frightened, sweat on his brow. "That's just . . . theoretically speaking . . . Yet your mother . . . oh, no, it's absurd, impossible, it's nonsense! Isn't it, Karol? Karol, what do you think?"

Why was Fryderyk turning to Karol? If he was scared—why was he buttonholing Karol as well? He belonged, however, to those who call the wolf out of the forest because they do not want to call it out—the fear itself luring it, magnifying it, creating it. But having called out the wolf, he could not desist from teasing it, running wild with it. Consequently his consciousness was so reckless and tormenting that he himself knew it not as light but as darkness—it was, for him, a blind elemental force as much as an instinct, he didn't trust it, he felt he was in its power, and he didn't know where it was leading him. He was not a good psychologist, because he had too much intelligence and imagination—in his wide view of man there was room for everything—so he could just as well imagine Madame Amelia in any situation. In the afternoon Vaclav left to "arrange matters with the police," namely to cool their investigative attempts with a sizable bribe—because, if the authorities tried to figure things out, who knows where it would end. The funeral took place the following morning—shortened, clearly speeded up. The next day we went back to Poworna and Vaclav came with us, leaving the house in God's mercy. This didn't surprise me—I understood that at this time he didn't want to part with Henia. The carriage in which the ladies, with Hipolit and Vaclav, were traveling, went first, behind it the *britzka* driven by Karol, and in it myself and Fryderyk, and someone else: Józek.

We brought him along because we didn't know what else to do with him. Let him go? He was a murderer. And besides, Vaclav wouldn't let him go under any conditions, because the death had, as yet, not been dealt with, so things couldn't be left just like that . . . and, above all, he hoped to draw a different version of the death from him, more seemly and less scandalous. And so, at the foot of the front seat of our *britzka*, on straw, lay the blond juvenile murderer, and Karol, who was driving, had him under his feet—therefore, sitting sideways, he was resting his feet on the wedge-shaped front of the *britzka*. Fryderyk and I were—in the back. The *britzka* went up, it went down along the immobile undulation of the ground, the terrain opened up and closed in, the horses trotted in the hot smell of grain and in the dust. While Fryderyk, sitting in back, had in front of him the two of them together, in this and in no other configuration—while the four of us, in the *britzka* that rolled from one hill onto the next, also formed a fairly good configuration, a meaningful formula, a strange arrangement . . . and, as the silent journey progressed, the figure that we formed became more intrusive. Immense was Karol's diffidence, his boyishness knocked off balance, he grew haggard under the blows of those tragic events, and he was as quiet as could be, and also kindly and docile . . . he even contrived a black tie for himself. Yet the two of them were there, right in front of Fryderyk and in front of me, by half a meter, on the front seat of the *britzka*. We went on. The horses trotted. Fryderyk's face was by necessity turned toward them—so what did he perceive in them? The two forms of the same age were as if a single form, that's how tightly the brotherly bond of their age united them. Yet Karol sat there above the lying fellow, with his reins, with the whip, shod in boots, his pants pulled up high—there was neither sympathy nor understanding between them. Rather, it was the harshness of a boy toward a boy, the unfriendly and even hostile brutality that they are apt to feel toward each other, deep down, one toward the other. And one could see that Karol belonged to us, to Fryderyk and to me, he was with us, with people of his own class and against a colleague from the rabble over whom he stood guard. Yet we had them in front of us, and over the many hours of sandy road (which sometimes widened into a highway, soon to bore into limestone walls), they were both in front of us and this was somehow affecting them, creating something, determining something. . . . While there, farther on, appeared on the hills the carriage in which she was riding—the fiancée. The carriage appeared and disappeared, not letting us forget it, sometimes it wasn't there for a long time but then it would reappear—while the oblique squares of the fields and the ribbons of meadows threaded onto our journey, wound and unwound—and in this geometry, boring, trotting, sluggish, drowned in vistas, drooped Fryderyk's face, his profile close to mine. What was he thinking? What was he thinking? We were traveling behind the carriage, we were chasing the carriage. Karol, with the other dark-eyed man under his feet, cornflower-blue and golden, barefoot and unwashed, was as if undergoing a chemical change, though he was following the carriage as a star follows a star, but by now he was with a colleague—in a collegial fashion—clasped from below, he with the other, almost as if handcuffed, united by the boy within him with the other boy to such an extent that if they had begun to eat cherries together, or apples, I would have not been at all surprised. We moved on. The horses trotted. Yes, that's what Fryderyk must have been imagining—or this is what he imagined that I was imagining—his profile was close to mine, and I didn't know which one of us had initiated this. Nonetheless, after many, many hours of moving through the countryside we reached Poworna, the two buddies were already "together with regard to Henia," united with reference to her, solidified in this by the many hours of travel behind her and in front of us.

We placed the prisoner in an empty pantry with a barred window. His wounds were superficial—he could have escaped. Tired beyond words, we fell into bed, I slept through the night and morning with a heavy sleep, and the next day I was besieged by intangible impressions, intrusive like a fly circling around my nose. I couldn't catch this buzzing fly, escaping me constantly—what fly? This assailed me even before lunch when I began talking to Hipolit about some detail connected with our still-fresh experiences, but I could hear in his response an almost imperceptible change of tone—not that he treated me abrasively, but there was something like haughtiness, or contempt, or pride, as if he'd had enough, or as if he had more important troubles. Troubles more important than the murder? And then I caught something in Vaclav's voice—I don't know—something cold, marked as well by something like pride. Were they proud? Proud of what? The change in tone was as subtle as it was jarring, for how could Vaclav be putting on airs barely two days after her death?—and my sensitized nerves suddenly dictated a suspicion that somewhere in our sky a new center of pressure had formed and some other wind was blowing—but what sort of wind? Something was transforming itself. Something seemed to be changing direction. Not until the evening did these misgivings assume a more distinct form, and that happened when I saw Hipolit crossing the dining room and saying, also whispering: "It's a mess, by God, it's a mess!" Suddenly he sat on a chair, dejected . . . then he rose, ordered the horses harnessed, and drove away. Now I knew that something new was forcing its way here, still, I didn't want to ask, but in the evening, when I saw Fryderyk and Vaclav circling the yard, talking, I joined them in the hope of finding out what was squeaking in the grass. Nothing of the kind. They were again discussing the death from the day before yesterday—and in the same tone as before—it was a confidential chat, conducted in hushed voices. Fryderyk, his head bent, his gaze fixed on his shoes, was again poking into the murder, pondering this, considering that, analyzing, searching . . . until Vaclav, finally worn out, began defending himself, asking for a reprieve, letting it be known that this was tantamount to insensitivity! "What is?" Fryderyk asked. "How am I to understand this?" Vaclav begged for mercy. It's too fresh, he wasn't used to it yet, he couldn't grasp it, he knows it without knowing, it's all too sudden, it's terrible! It was then that Fryderyk pounced on his soul like an eagle.

The comparison may be too high-flown. But one could clearly see that he was pouncing—and that he was pouncing from on high. In what he was saying there was neither comfort nor mercy, on the contrary, there was a demand that the son drain the chalice of his mother's death to the last drop. Just as Catholics live through Christ's Golgotha minute by minute. He made it clear that he himself was not a Catholic. That he does not have even the so-called moral principles. That he is not virtuous. "So why, you'll ask" (he was saying) "and in the name of what, am I demanding that you drain it to the limit? My reply is that it's purely and simply in the name of evolution. Who is man? No one knows. Man is a puzzle (and this platitude appeared on his lips like something both embarrassing and sarcastic, like pain—both an angelic and a devilish abyss, more bottomless than a mirror). Yet we must (the "must" was intimate and dramatic), we must experience life more and more fully. This, you know, is inevitable. This is the necessity of our evolution. We are doomed to evolve. This law fulfills itself in the history of mankind as it does in the history of a single human being. Look at a child. A child is only the beginning, a child does not exist, a child is a child, namely, an introduction, a beginning. . . . And a young man (he almost spat out this word) . . . what does he know? What can he be conscious of . . . he . . . an embryo? While we?

"We?" He exclaimed. "We?!"

And then, as an aside:

"Your mother and I instantly and profoundly understood each other. Not because she was a Catholic. But because she was subject to an inner compulsion toward seriousness . . . she was not at all . . . not at all . . . frivolous. . . ."

He looked into Vaclav's eyes—something that until now had probably never happened, and it greatly confounded Vaclav—who, nonetheless, did not dare avert his gaze.

"She was reaching . . . into the heart of the matter."

"What am I to do?" Vaclav exclaimed, raising his hands. "What am I to do?!"

If he had been talking with anyone else he would not have allowed himself to exclaim or to raise his hands. Fryderyk took him by the arm and moved forward, while with the finger of his other hand he pointed ahead. "One must rise to the magnitude of the task!" he said. "Do what you want. But let it be nothing less scrupulous in its . . . in its seriousness."

Seriousness is the highest and most unrelenting requirement for maturity—no letup—nothing that even for a moment would ease the intensity of a gaze searching stubbornly for the heart of the matter. . . . Vaclav didn't know how to defend himself against this severity—for it was indeed severity. In its absence, he would have doubted the seriousness of such behavior and the sincerity of such gesturing that conveyed some kind of agitation . . . but this theater was happening in the name of a stern summons to undertake and fulfill the highest duty of full awareness—and this, in Vaclav's eyes, made Fryderyk irrefutable. Vaclav's Catholicism could not be reconciled with the wildness of atheism—to a believer atheism is wild—and Fryderyk's world was for him a chaos deprived of a ruler, and therefore of law, peopled solely by man's arbitrariness . . . and yet, a Catholic could not fail to respect a moral imperative, even though it surfaced on such wild lips. And besides, Vaclav shuddered to think that for him his mother's death might come to nothing—that he would not be equal to the drama, or to his love and veneration—and he was more afraid of his own mediocrity, which turned him into a decent lawyer "with a fine-tooth comb," than he was afraid of Fryderyk's godlessness. He was therefore clinging to Fryderyk's firm superiority, seeking its support, oh, no matter how, no matter with whom, anything to experience that death. To live through it! To extract everything from it! For that he needed a wild yet fixed gaze into the heart of the matter, and that special, terrible obstinacy of living through it.

"But what am I to do with this Skuziak?" he exclaimed. "Who is to be his judge, I ask you? Who is to sentence him? Do we have the right to lock him up? Well and good, we didn't hand him over to the police, that would have been impossible—but we can't hold him in the pantry for ever!"

He broached the subject with Hipolit the next day but got only a wave of his hand: "No point worrying about it! Not worth bothering one's head with it! Hold him in the pantry, hand him over to the police, or whip him and release him, let him go. It's all the same to me!" But when Vaclav tried to explain that Skuziak was his mother's killer, Hipolit got annoyed: "A killer? A shit-head kid, not a killer! Do what you want with him, leave me alone, I have other things on my mind." He simply didn't want to hear about it, one had the impression that the murder was important to him from one end—Amelia's corpse—but trivial from the other, the murderer. And besides, he was clearly preoccupied with another worry. Suddenly something occurred to Fryderyk, who was standing by the heating stove, he moved as if to speak, but he only murmured: "Ohooo! . . ." He didn't say it aloud. He murmured it. And since we were not prepared for a murmur it resounded more than if Fryderyk had spoken with a full voice—and thus murmuring he stood there with his murmur while we waited for him to say something more. He said nothing. Then Vaclav, who had already learned to follow the slightest change in Fryderyk, asked: "What is it, what do you mean?" The accosted man looked around the room.

"Well, yes, it doesn't matter about *that one* . . . we can do whatever we want . . . whatever anyone wants to. . . ."

"With which one?" Hipolit exclaimed, with inexplicable anger. "With which one?"

Fryderyk tried to explain himself, somewhat disconcerted.

"With the one, well, it's obvious which one! With him—it doesn't matter. Whatever one wants to. Whatever one feels like."

"Wait. Wait a minute. You said the same thing about my mother," Vaclav suddenly interjected. "That my mother could actually have . . . with a knife . . . because . . ." He fumbled over his words. To which Fryderyk said, with obvious embarrassment: "Nothing, nothing, I just . . . Let's not talk about it!"

What an actor! One could clearly see the seams of his game, he wasn't hiding them. But it was also noticeable how much it cost him, how he *truly* paled and trembled in its clutches. To me at least, it was obvious that he was trying to impart to the murder and the murderer the most drastic character—but perhaps he wasn't trying, perhaps this was a necessity stronger than he was, to which he was succumbing in pallor and fear. It was, of course, a game—but it was a game that was creating him and also creating the situation. As a result everyone felt awkward somehow. Hipolit turned and left. Vaclav fell silent. Yet the blows struck by the player reached them just the same, Józek in the pantry was becoming more and more difficult, and the atmosphere in general was as if poisoned with a particular yet obscure intention. (I knew to whom it pertained, at whom it was aimed . . .) Every evening Józek's wounds had to be washed, and Fryderyk, who knew something about first aid, did this—with Karol's assistance, while little Henia held the lamp. This was, again, an intervention as significant as it was degrading, the three of them bending over him, each with something in hand, which justified the bending over—Fryderyk held the cotton wool, Karol a bowl and a bottle with alcohol, and Henia held the lamp—but the bending of the three of them over the wounded thigh was somehow tearing itself free from the objects they were holding, it was simply bending over him, while the lamp shone. Afterward Vaclav would lock himself up with the boy and question him—in a conciliatory way or by threatening him—

but the boy's inferiority and his darkness, together with his country origins, made him behave like an automaton, he kept repeating the same thing, that she threw herself on him, that she bit him, so what was he supposed to do? And, having become used to the questions, he felt at home with the answers.

"Her ladyship was bitin' me. Here are the marks, can't y' see?"

When Vaclav would return from the interrogations, exhausted like after an illness, Henia would sit next to him and stay with him quietly, faithfully . . . keeping him company . . . while Karol set the table or looked at the pictures in some old magazine . . . and as I looked at her, trying to see her "with Karol," I rubbed my eyes, unable to find those thrills that were no longer thrilling me—I was renouncing my frenzy. There was nothing between them, nothing, nothing! She's only with Vaclav! But in that case, oh, how insatiable she was! What an appetite! What an awful craving! How greedily she was trying to take him in hand, like a man a young woman! Forgive me, I don't have anything bad in mind, I just want to say that she was after his spirit with an unrestrained lasciviousness—she desired his conscience—his honor, his moral accountability, his dignity and all the suffering connected with it were the object of her craving, she was a glutton for all of his seniority to the point that even his baldness was more alluring to her than his little mustache! But all this was, of course, in a passive way peculiar to her—she merely absorbed his seniority, cuddled up to him, kept him company. And she would surrender to the caress of his masculine hand, nervous and refined, already matured, she—the one who was also seeking seriousness in relation to the dramatic death that went beyond her young, corporal ineptness which was clinging to someone else's maturity! Accursed one! So, instead of being splendid with Karol (which she was capable of), she preferred to be a slut and to whore about with the attorney, cuddling up to his pampered ugliness! Whereas the attorney, in his gratitude, was quietly stroking her, while the lamp was shining. Thus a few days passed. One afternoon Hipolit informed us that a new person is expected, a Mr. Siemian, who will come for a visit. . . . And he murmured, looking at his fingernail: "He'll come for a visit."

And he closed his eyes.

We took note of this information, not asking any unnecessary questions. The glum resignation in his voice did not attempt to hide that behind the "visit" lurks a net that is enveloping us all, tying us together, and at the same time turning us into strangers to each other—a conspiracy. Everyone could say only as much as was permissible—the rest was a painful, brooding silence, and insinuations. But, in any case, for the past few days a palpable though distant threat was already disturbing the uniformity of our emotions after the tragic events in Ruda, while a heaviness, the heaviness that had been crushing us, shifted from the recent past to an immediate future that was dangerous. In the evening, in the rain, the kind that changes from fine to gusty and lashing and then into an all-night slosh, a cabriolet arrived, and, in the hallway door inadvertently left ajar, a tall gentleman loomed in an overcoat, hat in hand, he stepped forward, preceded by Hipolit with a lamp, and headed for the stairs to the second floor, where lodgings had been prepared for him. A sudden gust of air nearly knocked the lamp out of Hipolit's hands, a door slammed. I recognized him. Yes, I already knew this man by sight, though he didn't know me—and I suddenly felt in this house as if in a trap. I happened to know that this guy was now a big shot in the underground movement, a leader who had on his record more than one instance of breakneck bravery, and that he was wanted by the Germans. . . . Yes, this was him, and, if it was so, his entry into this house was the entry of recklessness, why, we were at the mercy of his good or bad graces, his bravery was not only his personal business, by endangering himself he was also endangering us, he could pull us in and entangle us—and indeed, if he were to demand anything we would be unable to refuse. Because the nation was uniting us, we were comrades and brothers—but this brotherhood was as cold as ice, here everyone was the tool of everyone else, and one was allowed to use everyone else most ruthlessly, for the common goal.

This man, then, so close to us and yet so dangerously a stranger, passed before me like a looming threat, and from now on everything bristled and became suppressed. I was familiar with the danger he was bringing here, and yet I couldn't free myself from a distaste for this whole scenario—action, underground, leader, conspiracy—as if taken from a bad novel, like a belated embodiment of a bad, youthful daydream—and I truly would have preferred to have anything but this as a spoke in our wheel, at this moment our nation and all the romanticisms connected with it were for me an unbearable concoction, as if contrived intentionally, out of spite! Yet it wouldn't do to pick and choose and to disregard what fate was dishing out. I met "the leader" when he came down to supper. He looked like an officer, which he actually was—a cavalry officer, from eastern Poland, from the Ukraine perhaps, over forty years old, his face dark from shaving and dry, he was elegant, even gallant. He greeted everyone—it was obvious that this was not his first time here—he kissed the ladies' little hands. "Oh, yes, I know, how unfortunate! And you gentlemen are from Warsaw? . . ." From time to time he half-closed his eyes, giving the appearance of someone who's been a long time traveling, traveling by train. . . . They seated him at one of the farther places, supposedly he was here in the capacity of a technician, or a civil servant for cattle administration, or for planning crop planting—this was a necessary precaution because of the servants. As far as we, seated at the table, were concerned, it was at once apparent that everyone was more or less informed—though the conversation dragged sleepily and listlessly. But at the end of the table strange things were happening, namely with Karol, yes, with our (young) Karol, who had been thrown into an intense, willing obedience and eager readiness by the newcomer's presence—and, consumed with loyalty, his wits sharpened, suddenly he found himself close to death, a guerrilla, a soldier, a conspirator about whose hands and shoulders roamed a murderous yet quiet power, who was at Siemian's beck and call like a dog, obediently adroit, technically skillful. He wasn't the only one, however. I don't know whether it was his doing, but all the paltriness, so irritating and dreamy-eyed a moment earlier, was suddenly restored to health, in our banding together we arrived at reality and power, and at this table we were like a squad awaiting orders, already thrown into the possibility of action and battle. Conspiracy, action, enemy . . . this became a reality more powerful than our everyday life and blew in like a refreshing wind of sorts, Henia's and Karol's irksome otherness disappeared, we all began to feel like comrades. And yet this fraternization was not pure! No . . . it was also tormenting, even disgusting! Because, in God's truth, weren't we, the elders, a bit comical and somewhat repulsive in this battle—as happens in the case of love at an advanced age—was this appropriate to us, to Hipolit's bloating, to Fryderyk's skinniness, to Madame Maria's debility? The military unit that we formed was a unit of reservists—and our alliance was an alliance in decay—and despondency, surliness, abhorrence, and disgust hovered over our fraternization in fight and fervor. Yet at times it seemed wonderful that our fraternization, our fervor, were possible in spite of everything. But also, at times, I felt like calling out to Karol and to Henia, oh, separate from us, don't associate with us, avoid our dirt, our farce! But they (she included) were clinging to us—and pressing into us—and wanting to be with us—and surrendering to us, they were at our command, at our beck and call, ready to stand in our stead, for us, at the leader's beckoning! So it went all through supper. This is how I sensed it. Was I the one who sensed it this way, or was it Fryderyk?

Who knows, perhaps one of mankind's darkest mysteries—and the most difficult—is actually the one that pertains to this "uniting" of age groups—the manner and course by which youth suddenly becomes accessible to older age and vice versa. The key to the puzzle was in this case the officer, who, being an officer, had by this very fact a leaning toward a soldier and a young one at that . . . which became more apparent when, after supper, Fryderyk suggested to Siemian that he should check up on the killer in the pantry. As far as I was concerned, I didn't believe this was a random suggestion, I knew that Józek-killer-young-fellow's sojourn in the pantry had began to exert its pressure and became intrusive from the moment Karol surrendered to the officer. We went there—Siemian, Fryderyk, I, Henia, and Karol with the lamp. There he was, in the little room secured with bars, lying on the straw—curled up and asleep—and when we stood over him he moved, and in his sleep he covered his eyes with his hand. Childlike. Karol shone his lamp on him. Siemian signaled with his hand not to wake him. He eyed him as Madame Amelia's murderer, and yet Karol lit him up not as a murderer—but rather as if he were showing him to the leader—not so much as a murderer but as a young soldier—as if he were showing him as a colleague. And he was lighting him up almost as a recruit, as if this were a conscription . . . while Henia stood right behind Karol and watched as he was lighting him up. This struck me as something singular and on all accounts worthy of attention, that this was a soldier lighting up a soldier for an officer—there was something collegial and brotherly between them, the soldiers, yet cruel as well, yet giving him over as prey. And it seemed even more significant that it was a young one lighting up another young one for the older one—though I didn't quite grasp its meaning. . . .

In the pantry with its barred window a mute explosion of those three occurred around the lamp and in its glare—they exploded noiselessly with an unknown meaning, discrete yet eager. Siemian imperceptibly encompassed them with his gaze, it was only a moment, but long enough for me to learn that all this was not entirely foreign to him.

IX

Have I already mentioned that four small islands, separated by canals green with duckweed, made up the farther extent of the pond? Small bridges had been thrown over the canals. A lane at the very end of the garden, winding through a thicket of hazelnut bushes, jasmines, and arborvitae, allowed one to cross this archipelago, soggy with standing water. Walking there I imagined that one of the islands was not the same as the others. . . . Why? . . . a fleeting impression, but the garden had already been pulled into play too much to ignore this impression. . . . However . . . nothing. The day had been hot and it was teatime, the canal was almost dry and glistened with a crust of slime with its green eyes of water—brush was overgrowing the banks. Given our situation, any strangeness had to undergo immediate inspection, so I worked my way to the other shore. The little island breathed with heat, the grass was rampant, green and high, abundant with ants, and high above were the crowns of trees with their own, closed-off existence. I crept through the thicket and . . . Wait a minute. Wait! A surprise!

There was a bench. On the bench, she was sitting with her incredible legs—one of her legs was shod and in a stocking while the other was bare all the way above her knee . . . and this wouldn't have been so incredible, were it not for the fact that he, lying down, lying in front of her, on the grass, also had one leg bare and his pants leg pulled up above his knee. His shoe was nearby, a sock inside it. Her face and eyes were turned sideways. He was not looking at her, his arm around his head on the grass. No, no, all this would not have been so shocking, perhaps, if it had not been so incompatible with their natural rhythm, it was frozen, strangely immobile, as if it did not belong to them . . . and those legs, so strangely bared, only one from each pair, shining with their corporality in the humid, hot dampness interrupted by the splashing of frogs! He with a bare leg and she with a bare leg. Perhaps they had been wading in the water . . . no, there was more to it, this was beyond explanation . . . he with a bare leg and she with a bare leg. Her leg moved slightly, then stretched. She rested her foot on his foot. Nothing more.

I watched. Suddenly my total stupidity became apparent. Oh, oh! How could I have been so naive—and Fryderyk too—to think that "there was nothing" between them . . . to be seduced by appearances! Here I had a flat refutation right in front of me, like a blow to the head! So it was here that they had been meeting, on the island. . . . A gigantic scream, liberating and satisfying, resounded silently from this place—as their contact was maintained without motion, without sound, without even a gaze (because they weren't looking at each other). He with a bare leg and she with a bare leg.

Well and good . . . But . . . This could not be. There was an artificiality about it, something disturbing, something perverse. . . . What was the origin of this torpor, as if a spell had been cast? Where did the chill in their passion come from? For a fraction of a second I had a totally crazy thought *that this is how it should be, that this is how it should be between them*, that this is more real than if . . . Nonsense! And right away another thought came to me, namely, there's a funny game hiding here, a comedy, perhaps they had somehow found out that I'd be passing through here, and they were doing this on purpose—for my benefit. Because indeed this seemed to be for my benefit, exactly cut to the measure of my shame, of my daydreaming about them! For me, for me, for me! Spurred on by this thought—that it's for me—I tore through the bushes, disregarding everything. And then the picture became complete. Fryderyk was sitting under a pine tree on a pile of needles. This was—for him!

I stopped. . . . He, on seeing me, said to them:

"You'll have to repeat it once more."

And then, even though I had not yet understood anything, the chill of young lasciviousness blew from them. Depravity. They didn't move—their young freshness was terribly cold.

Fryderyk walked up to me, all gallantry. "Oh! How are you, my dear Mr. Witold! (The greeting was unnecessary, we had parted only an hour ago.) "What do you say about this pantomime?" (and with a sweeping gesture he pointed in their direction). "Not a bad performance, what, ha, ha, ha!" (the laughter was also unnecessary—loud as it was). "Where there's no fish, a crawfish is as good as fish! I don't know if you are familiar with my weakness for directing? I was also an actor for a while, I don't know if you are familiar with this detail of my biography?"

He took me under the arm and led me in a circle on the lawn, gesticulating in a theatrical manner. The others watched us without a word. "I have an idea . . . for a screenplay . . . a film screenplay . . . but some scenes are a bit risky, need work, one has to experiment with living material.

"That's enough for today. You may get dressed."

Not looking back at them, he led me away over the bridges, recounting loudly, with animation, his various ideas. In his opinion, the method, up to the present, for writing plays or screenplays "separate from the actor" was totally obsolete. One should begin with actors by "composing them together" in some manner, and building the theme of a play using these compositions. Because a play "should bring out only that which is already potentially inherent in the actors as living people who have their own range of possibilities." An actor "should not personify an imaginary stage hero and pretend to be someone he is not—on the contrary, the stage persona should conform to him, be cut to his measure, like a garment." "I'm trying," he was saying and laughing, "to achieve something like this with those kids, I promised them a little gift, because it's work, after all! Hey, you know, a man gets bored in this godforsaken countryside, one has to occupy oneself with something for the sake of health, if nothing else, Mr. Witold, for health! Of course I prefer not to make a show of it because—I don't know—perhaps it's too daring for a good fellow like Hipolit and his Mrs., I wouldn't want to expose myself to gossip! . . . " He was talking thus, loudly, so it would resound, while I, walking beside him and looking at the ground, the burning conundrum of this discovery in my head, hardly listened. The slyboots! The schemer! The fox! He was turning out such marvels—he had contrived such fun and games! . . . And everything was hurling down into cynicism and perversity, while the fire of this depravity was now consuming me, and, plainly, I was writhing in the throes of envy! And the glowing lights of my red-hot imagination lit up their chilly licentiousness, innocently devilish—especially hers, hers—for it was astounding that the faithful fiancée would go into the bushes for such séances . . . in return for the promise of a "little gift." . . .

"It's really an interesting theatrical experiment, of course," I responded, "yes, yes, an interesting experiment!" And I left him with all haste so that I could consider this further—because the depravity was surely not theirs alone and, as it turned out, Fryderyk had been managing things more successfully than I had thought—he was even able to get at them so directly! He was on his tack, ceaselessly. And this behind my back, on his own initiative! His pathetic rhetoric, which had unfolded with Vaclav upon Madame Amelia's death, didn't get in his way—he was in action—and the question was: how far had he gone on this road? And where would he still go? As far as he was concerned the problem of boundaries was becoming a burning issue—especially since he was pulling me along as well. I was scared. It was evening again—and with it the barely perceptible fading of light, the deepening and saturation of the darker hues, as well as the intensification of nooks and crannies that the night's sauce was filling. The sun was already behind the trees. I remembered having left a book on the porch, so I went to get it. . . . In the book I found an envelope without an address and in it a piece of paper with a note scrawled in pencil:

I'm writing this in order to be in communication with you. I don't want to be in this business totally alone, by myself, a lone player.

When one is alone one cannot have the certainty that, for instance, one hasn't gone mad. When there are two people—it's another matter. A twosome provides certainty, an objective guarantee. When there are two there's no madness!

I'm not really afraid of this. Since I know I couldn't go mad. Even if I wanted to. It's impossible for me, I'm an anti-madman. I want to secure myself against something else, possibly more serious, that is, I would say, against an Anomaly, a manifold increase of possibilities that comes about when man distances himself and goes off on the only possible, permissible road. . . . Do you understand? I don't have time for a more precise statement. If I were making a trip from the earth to some other planet, or merely to the moon, I would still prefer to be with someone—just in case, so that my humanity could mirror itself in something.

I will write from time to time, to keep you up to date. This is strictly confidential—unofficial—a secret even between ourselves, that is, burn this piece of paper, do not discuss this with anyone, not even with me. As if nothing has happened. Why upset—someone else, or oneself? It's best to avoid being demonstrative.

Actually it's good that you saw what you saw on the island. Better that two rather than just one should have seen this. Yet devil take all my labor, instead of exciting them and bringing them together, they were as cold as actors. . . . It was just for my sake, at my bidding, if anything, they are exciting themselves with me, not with each other! What bad luck! What bad luck! You know how it is because you saw it. But never mind. In the end we will inflame them.

You saw it, but now it's necessary that you should lure Vaclav. Let him see it! *Tell him that: (1) while walking about, you happened to see their* rendezvous *on the island, (2) you consider it your duty to inform him, (3) they don't know that you saw them. And tomorrow take him to the spectacle, the point is that he should see them and not see me, I'll figure out everything in detail and write, you'll receive my instructions. You must do it! It's important! As early as tomorrow! He must know, he must see it!*

Are you asking what my plan is? I have no plan. I walk the line of tensions, do you understand? I walk the line of excitements. Now I'm anxious to have him see it, and they should also know that they've been seen. We must lock them into the betrayal! Then we'll see what comes next.

Please take care of this. Please do not write back. I will be leaving my letters at the wall, by the gate, under a brick. Please burn the letters.

And that other one, that No. 2, that Józek, what is to be done with him, how, in what combination should he be combined with them so that everything works out, works out, after all he's perfect for the part, I'm racking my brains, I don't know anything, but slowly we'll sew it up, weave it together, let's just go forward, onward! Please carry out everything exactly.

The letter seared me! I began walking with it in my room, finally I went out with it into the fields—where the sleepiness of the swelling earth greeted me, as did the outline of the hills with the vanishing sky in the background and the increasing pre-nightfall onrush of all things. The landscape, already perfectly familiar, was just what I knew I would encounter here—but the letter put me off balance and away from any landscapes, oh, the letter put me off balance, and

I pondered what to do, what to do? What to do? Vaclav, Vaclav—on no account would I dream of doing this, it was well beyond what one does—and it is terrifying that the miasma of a preposterous lust was materializing into a fact, into a concrete fact that I had in my pocket, into a definite command. Had Fryderyk indeed gone mad? Was I necessary to him only so that his craziness could show its identity through me? This was indeed the last moment to break off with him—and I had before me a very simple solution. I could actually communicate with Vaclav and Hipolit . . . and already I saw myself talking to them: "Listen, this is an awkward matter. . . . I'm afraid that Fryderyk . . . is suffering from some mental problem. . . . I've been observing him for quite a while . . . well, after all those hellish experiences he's not the first and he won't be the last . . . but in any case we should pay attention to it, I think it's a kind of mania, an erotic mania, and it's actually directed toward Henia and Karol. . . ." That's what I would say. Each of those words would be casting him outside the orbit of healthy people, making him a madman—and all this could be done behind his back, turning him into an object of our discreet care and discreet supervision. He wouldn't know anything about it—and, being ignorant of it, he couldn't defend himself—he would be demon turned madman, and that would be it. While I would recover my balance. It was still not too late. I hadn't done anything yet that would embarrass me, the letter was the first embodiment of my cooperation with him. . . that's why it lay so heavily on me. So I had to decide—and, while returning to the house, and while the trees were diffusing into blotches shrouded in vagueness whose only meaning was darkness, I carried my resolve to render him harmless and to cast him out into the realm of simple lunacy. But the brick by the gate appeared white—I looked—there was already a new letter waiting for me.

The earthworm! You knew! You understood it! You had surely sensed it at the time, just as I did!

Vaclav is the worm! They have united on top of the worm. They will unite on top of Vaclav. By trampling Vaclav.

They don't want it with each other? They don't? You'll see that we will soon make a bed of Vaclav for them in which they will mate.

One must definitely stick Vaclav into this, he must (1) see it. T.b.c. To be continued.

I took the letter upstairs, to my room, which was where I read it. It was humiliating that its contents were so clear—as if I had written it to myself. Yes, Vaclav was to be the worm squashed by them jointly, to provide them the sin, to turn them into sinners, to cast them into the heat of the night. What was it, what was actually in the way, why DID THEY NOT WANT IT with each other? Oh, I knew—but I did not know—it was obvious yet elusive—it was as if they were youthfully escaping adult thinking . . . but in any case it was a kind of restraint, a kind of morality, a law, yes, an internal prohibition which they were obeying . . . so perhaps Fryderyk was not mistaken in thinking that when they trample Vaclav together, when they become depraved through Vaclav, this is precisely what will loosen them up! When they become lovers for Vaclav . . . they will become lovers for themselves. And for us, who are already too old, this is the only way of erotically coming closer to them. . . . Thrust them into this betrayal! When they find themselves in it together with us, there will be a mingling and unification! I understood that! And I also knew that sin will not spoil their beauty, on the contrary, their youth and freshness will be more powerful when they become black, pulled by our overripe hands into decay and united with us. Yes! I knew it! Enough of youth, merely meek and charming—this was about creating a different kind of youth, tragically permeated by us, the elders.

Enthusiasm. Wouldn't this fill me with enthusiasm? Well of course, no doubt about it. I, who was past my time of beauty, excluded from the glittering web of charisma—uncharismatic myself, unable to win people's hearts, uninteresting to nature . . . ha, I was still able to experience delight, yet I knew that my delight would never again be delightful . . . and so I was participating in life like a beaten dog, a mangy dog. . . . However, when at my age arises a chance of brushing against florescence, of entering into youth, even at the risk of depravity, and when it turns out that ugliness can be utilized, soaked up by beauty . . . It's a temptation that annihilates resistance, becomes utterly irresistible! Enthusiasm, yes, even a strangling passion—but on the other hand . . . And yet! Of course! But no! This is too crazy! It's not done! It's too much my own—too private and individual—and without precedent! And to enter on this demonic, separate road, with him, with a being that scared me since I sensed it as extreme, I knew it would take me too far!

And, was I, like Mephistopheles, to destroy Vaclav's love? No, oh, infamous and stupid fantasy! It's not my way! Not for the world! What then? Back out, go to Hipolit, to Vaclav, make a clinical case of it, transform the devil into a madman, hell into a hospital . . . and I was on the verge of taking a tight hold, with forceps, of the lasciviousness that was prowling about. Prowling? But where? What is he doing at this very moment? The fact that at this moment he is doing something—something I don't know about—brought me to my feet like a spring, I went outside, dogs surrounded me—no one about, only the house from which I had just emerged came into being in front of me and stood next to me, like an object. The kitchen windows were lit. Siemian's window (I had forgotten about him) was on the second floor. I was in front of the house, suddenly pierced by the distance of the starlit firmament and lost among trees. I vacillated, I swayed, farther on there was a gate, a brick nearby, I went to it, I went as if carrying out my duty, and when I was near it, I looked around . . . to see if he was lurking somewhere in the bushes. Under the brick—a new letter. What a writing spree!

Do you have a good, clear understanding?

I have already found out something.

(1) A PUZZLE: why not with each other? . . . What, hm? Do you know?

I know. It would have been too BRIMFUL for them. Too COMPLETE.

INCOMPLETENESS—FULLNESS, that's the key!

Almighty God! You are the Fullness! But this is more beautiful than You, O Lord, and I hereby renounce You.

(2) PUZZLE: why are they clinging to us? Why are they flirting with us?

Because what they want between themselves is through us. Us. And also—through Vaclav. Through us, Mr. Witold, my dear man, us, us. They must, through us. That's why they are courting us!

Have you ever seen anything like it? That they need us for this?

(3) Do you know what is so dangerous? That, in the fullness of my spiritual-intellectual development, I'm finding myself in hands that are lightweight, incomplete, only just growing up. O God! They are still growing! They will lightly, lightly, superficially lead me into something that I will have to totally exhaust *intellectually and emotionally. They will*

present me a chalice, lightly-thoughtlessly, and I will have to drain it to the last drop. . . .

I always knew that something like this was awaiting me. I am Christ, stretched on a sixteen-year-old cross. Bye-bye! Till I see you on Golgotha. Bye-bye!

What a writing spree! I was again sitting by a lamp in my room upstairs: should I betray him? Denounce him? But in that case I would also have to betray and denounce myself!

Myself too!

This was not entirely his alone. It was mine too. But to make a fool of myself? To betray within me the only chance of entering, entering . . . into what? Into what? Into what?! What was it? They called me for supper from downstairs. When I found myself in the everyday arrangement that we had formed at the table, all matters surrounding us, the war and the Germans, the countryside and our troubles, returned and hit me . . . but they hit me as if from some remote place . . . and they were no longer my own.

Fryderyk was also sitting here, at his place—and he carried on at length, while eating cheese dumplings, about the situation at the front. And he turned to me several times, asking for my opinion.

X

Vaclav's initiation went strictly according to plan. Nothing unforeseen complicated the initiation, its course was smooth and calm.

I said "I want to show you something." I took him to the canal, to the appointed spot from which one could view the scene through a gap between the trees. At this spot in the canal the water was deep—this functioned as a necessary safeguard so he couldn't force his way to the island and discover Fryderyk's presence.

I showed him.

The scene that Fryderyk had devised in his honor was as follows: Karol under a tree, she just behind him, their heads raised high, watching something on a tree, perhaps a bird. He raised his hand. She raised her hand.

Their hands, high above their heads, intertwined "unintentionally." And, upon intertwining, they yielded to a downward pull, fast and sudden. For a moment, lowering their heads, they watched their hands. Then, without warning, they fell, it wasn't actually clear who toppled who, it seemed it was their hands that had toppled them.

They fell and for a moment, lay together, and then sprang quickly to their feet . . . again they stood, as if not knowing what to do. Slowly she walked away, he followed her, they disappeared behind the bushes.

A scene ingenious in its apparent simplicity. In this scene the simplicity of the union of hands suffered an unexpected shock—the fall to the ground—its naturalness went through an almost convulsive complication, a veering from the norm so sudden that for a second they were like marionettes in the throes of an elemental force. But this was only a moment, and their coming to their feet, their calm walking away made one guess that they were already used to it. . . . As if this was not happening for the first time. As if it was familiar to them.

The stench of the canal. Sultry dampness. Immobile frogs. It was five in the afternoon, the garden was weary. The heat.

"Why did you bring me here?"

He asked this as we were returning home.

I replied.

"I considered it my duty."

He pondered.

"Thank you."

When we were close to the house he said: "I don't think . . . that this is of major significance. . . . But in any case, thank you for bringing it to my attention. . . . I'll have a talk with Henia."

Nothing more. He went to his room. I was left alone, disappointed, as is always the case when something comes to fulfillment—because fulfillment is always murky, insufficiently clear, devoid of the greatness and purity of the undertaking. After completing the task I suddenly became unemployed—what should I do with myself?—emptied as I was of the fact to which I had given birth. It was getting dark. Again it was getting dark. I went onto the field and walked along a path, my head lowered, just to keep walking, the ground beneath my feet was ordinary, silent and friendly. On my return I looked under the brick but nothing was awaiting me, only the brick—cool and darkened by dampness. I marched down the road across the courtyard to the house and stopped, unable to enter it, to enter into the ambit of matters taking place there. And yet, at the same time, the sweltering heat of their interweaving, of their precocious and awakened blood, of their intertwining and embracing, fell onto me with such fervor that I broke through the door and rushed into the house to continue realizing our business! I barged in! But here awaited me one of those sudden turns which, at times, catch you by surprise. . . .

Hipolit, Fryderyk, and Vaclav were in the study—and they called me.

Suspecting that their session related to the scene on the island, I approached them warily . . . but something warned me that this was something from a different barrel. Hipolit was sitting behind his desk, glum, and he was staring at me.

Vaclav was pacing the room. Fryderyk was half-lying on an armchair. Silence. Vaclav said:

"We have to tell Mr. Witold."

"They want Siemian liquidated," Hipolit said somewhat cursorily.

I still didn't understand. An explanation soon ensued that placed me in a new situation—and, once more, a theatrical pattern of patriotic conspiracy wafted in—perhaps even Hipolit was not free of it, since he began to speak harshly, almost sneeringly. And sternly. I learned that during the night Siemian "saw certain persons who had arrived from Warsaw" for the purpose of settling details of an action that he was to carry out in this area. But in the course of that conversation something happened "a nasty business, you know," Hipolit added, because Siemian apparently said that he will no longer conduct either this or any other action, that he is withdrawing from the resistance once and for all, and that he is "going home." Nasty business indeed! There was an uproar, they began pressuring him, until finally, nervously, he spat out that he had done what he could and could do no more—that "his courage had come to an end"—that "his courage had changed into fear"—he said "leave me in peace, something's gone bad, fear has taken root within me, I myself don't know how"—that he was no longer fit for anything, that it would be sheer recklessness to entrust him with anything under these conditions, that he was dutifully forewarning them about it and asking for his release. This was all too much. In the fierce exchange of nervous opinions a suspicion began to arise, at first unclear, then more and more sharply defined, that Siemian had gone mad, or, at the very least, had completely lost his nerve—and then a wave of panic hit, that a certain other secret that had been placed with him was not safe, one could no longer be sure he wouldn't spill the beans . . . and, because of certain incidental circumstances, all this took the form of a catastrophe, of defeat, of the end of the world almost, and thus with this escalation, pressure, tension, there emerged a frightened and frightening decision to kill him, to liquidate him immediately. Hipolit recounted that they had wanted to follow Siemian right away into his room and shoot him—but that he, Hipolit, begged for a delay until the following night, explaining that one had to work out the matter logistically, bearing in mind our, the household's, safety. They agreed to a delay of no longer than twenty-four hours. They were afraid that Siemian would sense that he was in danger and would escape. Poworna was actually well suited for their design, since Siemian had arrived here in great secrecy and no one would look for him here. It was settled that they would return tonight to "do the job."

Why did the reality of our fight with the enemy and the invader have to appear in such vivid attire—and to such a highly infuriatingly humiliating degree!—as in bad theater—even though there was blood in this, there was death, and it was most real? "What is he doing now?" I asked in order to better grasp—to get used to the new situation. Hipolit offered me this response:

"Upstairs. In his room. He locked himself in. He asked for horses, he insists on leaving. Surely I can't provide him with horses."

And he murmured to himself:

"Surely I can't provide him with horses."

There was no doubt that he couldn't. On the other hand, one doesn't do the job just like that—finishing off a man without a court hearing, no formalities, no papers? But this was none of our business. We spoke like people besieged by disaster. However, when I asked what they were planning to do, I was met with an almost crude response. "What do you want? It's no use talking! It must be done!" Hipolit's tone of voice revealed a lightning-fast change in our relation. I ceased to be a guest, I was in service, stuck with them in harshness, in cruelty that was turning as much against us as against Siemian. But how had he wronged us? All of a sudden, rushing headlong, we had to butcher him, endangering our own necks.

"In the meantime there's no need for us to do anything. They are supposed to return at twelve-thirty. I sent our watchman away to Ostrowiec, supposedly for some urgent shopping, the dogs won't be off the leash. I'll just take the men to him, upstairs, they can do what they want. The only condition I stipulated was that they don't make noise or the entire household will be wakened. As to the body, it will be removed . . . I've already figured it out, to the shed. And tomorrow one of us will supposedly take Siemian to the railroad station, and that's that. It will all be on the quiet, smooth as can be, and not a living soul will know a thing."

Fryderyk asked: "In that old shed, behind the carriage house?"

He asked objectively, like a conspirator, like someone about to execute a plan—and, in spite of everything, I felt relieved seeing him so mobilized—like a drunkard who has been recruited to a cause. No more drinking for him, right? And all of a sudden this whole affair seemed to me like something healthy and much more decent than our activities thus far. But this relief did not last for long.

Right after supper (eaten in Siemian's absence, for the past few days he had been "indisposed"—food was sent to him upstairs) I went to the gate, just in case, and there, under the brick, was a white piece of paper.

There is a complication. It's thwarting our plans.

We must wait it out. Mum's the word.

We must see what's what. How events will unfold. If there is a hullabaloo and we have to flee, to Warsaw for instance, the others somewhere else, well, too bad—then everything will fall apart.

One must be familiar with the old wh . . . You know who I mean? She, i.e. Nature. If She pressures from the side with something so unexpected, one mustn't protest or resist, one must obediently, meekly adjust, "faire bonne mine" . . . *but don't let up inwardly, or lose sight of our goal, and in such a manner that She'll realize we have yet another goal, a goal of* our own. *To begin with She is sometimes v. determined in her interventions, decisive, etc., but then She seems to lose interest, lets up, and then one can covertly return to* one's own *work and even count on her leniency. . . . Attention! Adjust your behavior in keeping with mine. So there is no discrepancy. I will write. You must burn this letter,* without fail.

This letter . . . This letter which, even more than the previous one, was the letter of a madman—yet I understood this madness perfectly. It was so intelligible to me! The *tactic* that he was pursuing in his relations with nature—indeed, it wasn't foreign to me! And he was clearly not letting his goal out of his sight, he had written in order not to give in, to underscore that he continues to be true to his undertaking, the letter, feigning submissiveness, was at the same time a call to resistance and stubbornness. And who knows whether it was written to me or to Her—so that she *would know* that we did not intend to back off—he was talking to Her through me. I was wondering whether Fryderyk's every word, as well as his every deed, only pretended to address the one to whom it was directed, while in reality there was indefatigably a dialogue with the Powers . . . a cunning dialogue, where lying was at the service of truth, truth—at the service of lying. Oh, how he feigned in this letter that he was writing in secrecy from Her—while in truth he was writing so that She would find out! And he was counting that his cunning would disarm Her—perhaps amuse Her. . . . We spent the rest of the evening waiting. Furtively we checked our watches. The lamp barely lit the room. Henia, as she did every evening, huddled by Vaclav, he, as usual, had his arm around her, while I discovered that "the island" had not changed his feelings in the least. Inscrutable, he sat next to her, while I racked my brains to see to what extent he was filled with Siemian, and to what extent Karol's noise and moving about were reaching him as Karol was turning things upside down in chests and tidying them up again. Madame Maria was sewing (like "the children," she had not been let into the secret). Fryderyk, his legs outstretched, his hands on the arms of an armchair. Hipolit on a chair, gazing into space. Our excitement was swathed in fatigue.

Kept apart by the business of Siemian, that secret task of ours, we men formed a separate group. Henia happened to ask Karol: "What on earth are you doing with that stuff, Karol?" "Don't bother me!" he replied. Their voices resounded *in blanco*—God knows what they meant and what their inexplicable activity was—while we didn't budge.

They went to bed around eleven o'clock, as did Madame Maria, while we men began to bustle about. Hipolit brought out shovels, a sack, ropes, Fryderyk put weapons in order just in case, while Vaclav and I carried out an inspection outside. Lights in the windows of the house were turned off, except the one on the second floor—Siemian's—that was shining through the curtain with a pale mist of light and dread, dread and light. How could it be that his courage had so suddenly changed into fear? What happened to this man that hurled him headlong into a breakdown? Changing from a leader into a coward? Well! Well! What an adventure! Out of the blue the house seemed to be filled with two separate possibilities of madness, Siemian's on the second floor, Fryderyk's on the first (carrying out his game with nature) . . . in some manner they were both pushed against the wall, at their wit's end. On my return to the house I almost burst out laughing at the sight of Hipolit, who was looking at two kitchen knives and trying their blades. O God! That venerable fatso, transformed into a murderer and preparing himself for butchering, was like someone in a farce—and suddenly our bungling uprightness, so inept and stuck into murder, turned all this into a performance by a troupe of amateurs, more amusing than menacing. It was actually being done *just in case,* it did not have a decisive character. Yet at the same time the knife's glint struck like something irrevocable: the die had already been cast, the knife has made its appearance!

Józek! . . . and Fryderyk's eyes, stuck on the knife, left no doubt what he was thinking. Józek . . . the knife . . . Identical to the other knife, Madame Amelia's, almost the same, and here it was with us—oh, this knife was connected to the other crime, called it to mind, it was, as it were, a repetition of it a priori—right here, right now, suspended in air—a strange analogy, to say the least, a significant repetition. The knife. Vaclav was also watching it intently—and so these two minds, Fryderyk and Vaclav, had caught up with the knife and were already working on it. They were actually on duty, in action—they locked it within themselves—as we devoted ourselves to preparations and waiting.

The job, we had to carry it out—but oh how tired we were already, disgusted with history's melodrama, longing for regeneration! After midnight Hipolit proceeded on the quiet to a meeting with the men from the Underground Army. Vaclav went upstairs to keep an eye on Siemian's door—I was left downstairs with Fryderyk, and never before had being alone with him weighed on me so heavily. I knew he had something to say—but talking was forbidden to us—so he remained quiet—and, although there was no one around and no one to eavesdrop, we behaved like strangers, and this caution actually called up from nothingness a third presence of an unknown quality, something intangible yet unrelenting. And his face—so familiar to me, the face of an associate—seemed to be walled off from me. . . . Next to each other we were next to each other, we just were and were, until we heard Hipolit's lumbering walk and heavy breathing return. He was alone. What happened? A complication! Something went wrong. Something got mixed up. Panic. Those who were supposed to show up didn't arrive. Someone else came and already left. "And as far as Siemian is concerned," Hipolit said, "well . . .

"Can't be helped, we'll have to take care of it ourselves. The others can't, they had to scram. Those are the orders."

What?! Yet from Hipolit's words a coercion, an order, pressed upon us, we are not to let him go under any pretence, especially now, when the fate of many people depends on it, we can't take risks, there are the orders, no, not in writing, there was no time, there just is no time, no use talking, it has to be done! These were the instructions to us! This is what the orders were like, brutal, panicky, created in a realm of tension unknown to us. To cast doubt on it? This would throw the responsibility for all the consequences onto us, and these could be catastrophic, surely they would not have resorted to such drastic measures without cause. And resistance on our part would look like searching for excuses—just when we were demanding total readiness from ourselves. Thus no one could allow anyone any semblance of weakness, and if Hipolit had led us to Siemian right then, we would have done the job from sheer momentum. But the unexpected complication gave us a pretext to postpone the action until the following night, roles had to be assigned, preparations made, safety assured . . . and it became clear that if things could be postponed, they should be postponed . . . so I was assigned to keep an eye on Siemian's door until daybreak, then Vaclav was to relieve me. We bade each other good night because, after all, we were well-mannered people. Hipolit withdrew to his bedroom, taking the lamp with him, we lingered a while by the stairs leading to the next floor, but then a figure slipped by through the dark suite of rooms. Vaclav had a flashlight, he shot out a bright ray of light. Karol. In his nightshirt.

"Where were you? What are you doing here at night?" Vaclav exclaimed softly, unable to control his nerves.

"I was in the bathroom."

This could be the truth. Indeed. Vaclav wouldn't have unexpectedly emitted such an intense groan but for the fact that he had exposed Karol with the light of his own flashlight. But having done so, he groaned loudly, almost indecently. He surprised us with this groan. Karol's coarse and challenging tone surprised us no less.

"What do you want?"

He was ready for a fight. The fiancé immediately switched off his flashlight. "I truly beg your pardon, we heard something in the darkness, I merely asked."

And he left quickly, in the dark.

I didn't have to put my head out of my room to keep watch on Siemian—there was only a wall between us. It was quiet at his place, though he had not turned off the lamp. I preferred not to go to bed for fear of falling asleep, I sat at my table, but the rhythm of the course of events was throbbing in my head, and I found it hard to cope with—because, above the material ebb and flow of facts, there hovered a mystic sphere of accents and meanings, like the sun's glare over a whirlpool. I sat like this for almost an hour, gazing into that glittering stream, until finally I noticed a piece of paper that had been awaiting me, stuck through a chink in the door.

A propos the latest W—K clash. That was quite a fury erupting. K. would have beaten him up!

They already know that he saw them. That's why.

They already know because I told them. I told them that you had told me that Vaclav had told you—that he saw them on the island by chance. That he saw them (but not me) while walking along the path, by chance.

As it's easy to guess, they burst out laughing, i.e., they burst out laughing together, *because I told them both at the same time, and they, being together, had to burst out laughing . . . because they were together and what's more, in front of me! Now they are FIXED as* laughing torturers *of W. That is, as long as she and Karol are together, coupled, as a couple—for you saw after all, at supper, she, by herself, i.e., on her own, remains his faithful fiancée. But together they are laughing at him.*

And now for the KNIFE.

The knife makes a compound S (Siemian)—S1 (Skuziak).

From this follows: (SS1)—W. Through A, through Ameila's murder.

What chemistry! How everything connects! These connections are still vague, but one can see there is a TENDENCY in that direction. . . . And imagine, I didn't know what to make of that Skuziak—while here he is, crawling in all by himself by way of the KNIFE. But be careful. Don't scare them away! One mustn't force anything . . . one mustn't impose, let's go with the current as if there's nothing afoot, and merely take advantage of every chance to get closer to our *goal.*

We must cooperate with Hipolit's underground activity. Don't let on that our underground activity is of a different kind. Behave as if you're stuck in the national struggle, in the Underground Army, in the Poland-Germany dilemma, as if this is what it's all about . . . while in reality our point is that

HENIA WITH KAROL

But we mustn't reveal this. We mustn't let on to anyone. No one. Not even to ourselves. Mum's the word. We mustn't put it forward—suggest it to anyone. Silence! Let it evolve by itself. . . .

We need courage and stubbornness, because we must stick to our purpose *even if it does look like lascivious swinishness. The swinishness will cease to be swinishness if we stick to it! We must press on, because, if we let up, the swinishness will drown us. Don't be thrown off balance—don't let on! There is no retreat.*

My greetings. Best regards. Burn this.

"Burn this" he commanded. But it had already been written. "THE POINT IS HENIA WITH KAROL . . ." Whom was this addressed to? To me? Or to Her, to nature?

Someone knocked on the door.

"Come in."

Vaclav entered.

"May I talk to you?"

I gave him my chair, which he took. I sat on the bed.

"I'm very sorry, I know you're tired. But I realized I won't be able to sleep a wink until I talk to you. In a different way than I have so far. More frankly. I hope you don't hold it against me. You probably know what it's about. About . . . about this thing on the island."

"There isn't much I can . . ."

"I know. I know. Forgive me for interrupting you. I know that you don't know anything. But I'd like to know what you're thinking. I'm having a hard time coping with my thoughts. What do you think about that? What do you—think?"

"Me? What can I think about it? I merely showed it to you, considering it my du . . ."

"Of course. I'm much obliged. I really don't know how to thank you. But I'd like to know your point of view. Perhaps I should state my view first. I think it's nothing. Nothing important—it's because they've known each other since childhood and . . . It's more silliness than . . . And at their age too! No doubt in years past there was . . . something between them . . . perhaps something half-childish, you know, teasing and intimacies, and it had acquired some more specific form—quirky, yes? And now they sometimes return to it. A beginning, a budding sensuality. One must also allow for an optical illusion because we were looking from a distance, from behind the bushes. I mustn't doubt Henia's feelings. I have no right to. I have no basis for it. I know she loves me. How could I ever compare our love to such . . . childishness. So nonsensical!"

Body! He sat directly across from of me. Body! He was in his bathrobe—he was here with his corpulent, pampered, plump and whitish, groomed and robed body! He sat with his body as if it were a suitcase, or a toiletry case. Body! I was furious at the body and, for that reason, carnal myself, I watched him mockingly, I was mocking for all I was worth, almost whistling. Not one iota of compassion. Body!

"You can believe me, or not believe me, but this really would not have upset me. . . . Except that . . . one thing is torturing me. I don't know, perhaps it's an illusion. . . . That's why I wanted to ask you. I beg your pardon in advance if it's a bit . . . far-fetched. I must admit that I don't know how to put it. What they were doing . . . you know, they fell so abruptly, then they rose . . . you must agree it was . . . somewhat peculiar. One doesn't do it *like that!*"

He fell silent and swallowed his saliva, and he was embarrassed that he was swallowing.

"Is that your impression?"

"It didn't happen normally. If they were kissing, you know—just simply . . . If he, let's say, knocked her off her feet—just simply. Even if he had simply taken her right before my eyes. All that would have . . . disconcerted me less . . . than this strangeness . . . the strangeness of their movements. . . ."

He took my hand. He looked into my eyes. I cringed with disgust. I hated him.

"Please tell me frankly, am I right? But perhaps I didn't see it as I should have? Perhaps it's my own quirkiness? I don't know myself. Please tell me!"

Body!

Scrupulously hiding my frivolous yet merciless maliciousness, I said—actually nothing much—nothing that would add oil to the fire: "I don't know. . . . Actually . . . Perhaps to some degree . . ."

"But I don't know what importance I should attach to it?! Is it something—significant? And to what extent? First of all tell me: do you think that she and he? . . ."

"What?"

"I'm sorry! I'm thinking of *sex appeal.* What we call *sex appeal.* When I saw them together for the first time . . . this was a year ago . . . it caught my eye right away. *Sex appeal.* Attraction. Sexual attraction. He and she. But at that time I wasn't serious about Henia. Later, when she aroused my feelings, that other thing moved to the background, compared with my feelings the other thing lost its meaning, I stopped paying attention to it. It was childish after all! But now . . ."

He took a deep breath.

"Now I'm afraid that it may be—worse than anything I could have imagined."

He rose.

"They fell to the ground . . . not as they normally would have. And they rose right away—also not quite normally. And also they left not quite normally. . . . What is it? What does it mean? One doesn't do it *like that!*"

He sat down.

"What? What? What's the point of it?"

He looked at me.

"Oh, how it twists my imagination! You tell me! Just tell me something! Don't leave me alone with this!" He smiled wanly. "Forgive me."

So this one was also seeking my company, preferring "not to be in this alone"—I was popular indeed! However, unlike Fryderyk, he was begging me not to have his madness confirmed and, with a trembling heart, he awaited my denial that would push everything into the realm of the chimerical. It was up to me—whether to calm him down. . . . Body! If only he talked to me solely as a soul! But the body! And this levity of mine! I didn't need to exert myself in order to settle him once and for all in hell, it was enough, as I had done before, to mumble a few indistinct words: "I must admit . . . Perhaps . . . It's hard to say . . . It's possible that . . . ," I said. He replied:

"She loves me, and I know beyond a doubt that she loves me, she loves me!"

He was defending himself, in spite of everything.

"She loves you? I don't doubt it. But don't you think that between them love is superfluous. With you she needs love, with him she doesn't."

Body!

He said nothing for a long while. He sat quietly. I too sat and said nothing. Silence enveloped us. What about Fryderyk? Was he asleep? And Siemian? And Józek in the pantry? How about him? Is he asleep? The house seemed to be harnessed to many horses, each one pulling in a different direction.

He smiled, embarrassed.

"This is really unpleasant," he said. "I just lost my mother. And now . . ."

He thought for a while.

"I really don't know how to apologize for this nocturnal intrusion. I was—beside myself. I want to tell you one more thing, if you'll permit me. I'm anxious that it be said. What I will tell you will be . . . Well. Listen. I'm often surprised that she . . . feels something for me. As far as my feelings are concerned—that's a different matter. I feel what I feel for her because she's created for love, she is for love, to be loved. Yet what is it that she loves in me? My feelings, my love for her? No, not just that, she also loves *me for myself*—but why? What does she love in me? You know what I'm like. I have no illusions, I don't like myself much, and I really don't know, I can't understand what she sees in me, I admit it even offends me. If I have anything to reproach her for, it's exactly that she . . . accepts me so graciously. Would you believe it, that in moments of the most passionate ecstasy I resent this very ecstasy, the fact that she succumbs to it with me? And I have never been able to feel at ease with her, it has always felt like a favor, a concession granted me, I even had to summon up cynicism in order to take advantage of this "convenience," this kindhearted arrangement created by nature. Well and good. All in all—she loves me. That's a fact. Undeserved or deserved, convenient or inconvenient, she loves me."

"She loves you. Undoubtedly."

"Wait! I know what you want to say: that theirs is outside love, in another realm. True! That's why this affair that's happening to me is . . . immorally barbarous, exceptionally fanciful in its maliciousness—it's hard to understand how by some devilish miracle this could have happened. If she were to be unfaithful to me with a grown man . . .

"My fiancée is running around with someone like this," he suddenly said with a different tone of voice and looked at me. "What does this mean? And how am I to defend myself? What am I to do?

"She's running around with someone outside . . . ," he elaborated, "and in a manner that's strange . . . unique . . . unheard of . . . one that touches, permeates me, you know, because I taste its flavor, I grasp its . . . Would you believe that on the basis of this sample that we watched, I have mentally reconstructed *everything* that is possible between them, the totality of their relation. And this is so . . . erotically brilliant, that I don't know how they happened upon it! It's like something out of a dream! Which one of them thought it up? He or she? If it was her—then she's quite an artist!"

After a moment.

"And you know what I think? That she didn't give herself to him. And this is more awful than if they were sleeping together. Such a thought is sheer madness, isn't it? Indeed! Because, if she had given herself to him I could defend myself, but this way . . . I can't . . . and it's possible that she, by not giving herself to him, is even more his. Because everything between them is happening differently, differently! It's something different! It's something different!"

Ha! There was one thing he didn't know. Namely, that what he saw on the island was happening *for* Fryderyk and *through* Fryderyk—it was a kind of bastard child, created by them with Fryderyk. And what satisfaction—to keep him in ignorance, he, not having a clue that I, his confidant, am on the other side, with the elemental force that is destroying him. Even though this was not my elemental force (because it was too young). Even though I was his contemporary, not theirs—and by ruining him I was actually ruining myself. Yet—what wonderful levity!

"It's because of the war," he said. "It's because of the war. But why do I have to carry on a war with those kids? One of them killed my mother, and the other . . . This is too much, a little bit too much. It's going too far. Do you want to know how I'll conduct myself?"

Since I didn't answer, he repeated with emphasis.

"Do you want to know how I will act?"

"I'm listening. Tell me."

"I won't back down an inch."

"Aha!"

"I won't let her be seduced—nor be seduced myself."

"What do you mean?"

"I know how to hang on to what's mine and how to keep my eye on it. I love her. She loves me. This is the only important thing. The rest must give way, the rest must be of no significance, because that's how I want it. I'm capable of wanting it. You know, I don't actually believe in God. My mother was a believer. I'm not. But I want God to exist. I want it—and this is more important than if I were merely convinced of his existence. And in this case I'm also capable of wanting it and I will hold my ground, my morality. I'll call Henia to order. So far I haven't spoken to her, but early tomorrow I'll have a word with her, I'll call her to order."

"What will you tell her?"

"I'll behave decently, and I'll force her into decency. I'll act with respect—I'll treat her with respect and I'll force her to respect me. I'll deal with her in such a way that she won't be able to refuse her affection and fidelity to me. I believe that respect, reverence, you know—create obligation. And I'll treat that brat to his due. Now, recently, he made me lose my composure—it won't happen again."

"You want to act . . . with importance?"

"You took the words out of my mouth! Importance! I'll call them to—what's important!"

"Yes, but 'importance' derives from 'import.' A man of importance deals with what is most important. What then is most important? For you one thing can be the most important, for them—another. Everyone chooses according to his judgment—and his measure."

"What do you mean? I'm the important one, they're not. How can they be important when these are childish things—rubbish—nonsense. Idiotic things!"

"But what if—for them—childishness is more important?"

"What? Whatever is important to me has to be more important to them. What do they know? I know better! I'll force them! You can't deny that I'm surely more important than they are, it's my argument that must be the decisive one."

"Wait a minute. I thought you considered yourself more important because of your principles . . . but now it appears that your principles are more important because you yourself are more important. Personally. As a person. As an elder."

"Club it or cudgel it!" he exclaimed, "it's all the same thing! I'm very sorry. These confidences at such a late hour. I thank you very much."

He left. I felt like laughing. Well, what a lark! He swallowed the hook—he was thrashing about like a fish!

What a trick our little couple had played on him!

Was he suffering? Suffering? Well, yes, he was suffering, but it was a pudgy kind of suffering—weary—balding. . . .

The charm was on the other side. So I was "on the other side" too. Everything that came from there was—delightful and . . . skilled in enticement . . . endearing . . . Body.

That bull, who was pretending to defend morality, was in reality bearing down on them with all his weight. Bearing down on them with his very self. He was inflicting on them that morality of his for no other reason than that it was his "own"—it carried more weight, was older, more developed . . . the morality of a grown man. Inflicting it by force!

What a bull! I couldn't stand him. The only thing . . . wasn't I just like him? I—a grown man . . . I was thinking about that when I again heard a knocking on my door. I was sure it was Vaclav returning—but it was Siemian! I began coughing in his face—I did not expect this!

"Forgive me for troubling you, but I heard voices, so I knew you weren't asleep. May I ask you for a glass of water?"

He drank slowly, in small sips, not looking at me. Without a tie, his shirt open, his features wrinkled—his hair, though pomaded, was sticking up and he fingered it from time to time. He drained the glass but was not leaving. He stood fingering his hair.

"What an arabesque!" he mumbled. "Unbelievable! . . . " He went on standing as if I weren't there. Purposely I said nothing. He said under his breath, not to me:

"I need help."

"What can I do for you?"

"You know that I'm having a total nervous breakdown?" he asked indifferently, as if this did not apply to him.

"I must admit . . . I don't understand."

"Yet you must be au courant," he laughed. "You know who I am. And that I have broken down."

He was brushing out his hair and waiting for my response. He could have waited indefinitely, since he was deep in thought, or rather he was concentrating on a thought while not thinking. I decided to find out what he wanted—I replied that indeed I was au courant. . . .

"You're a nice man. . . . I just couldn't stand it in my room any longer . . . in isolation. . . ." he pointed to his room with his finger. "How shall I put it? I decided to turn to someone. I decided to turn to you. Perhaps because you're a nice man, or perhaps because you're next door. . . . I can no longer be alone. I can't and that's that! May I sit down?"

He sat down, while his movements were as if he had been ill—cautious, as if he didn't have full control over his limbs and had to plan each move ahead. . . . "I'd like to ask you for some information," he said. "Is there something being schemed against me?"

"Why?" I asked.

He decided to laugh, then he said: "Forgive me, I'd like to be frank . . . but first I need to make it clear in what role I'm appearing before you, dear sir. I'll have to give you some account of my life. Please be kind enough to listen. You probably know a lot about me from hearsay. You've heard of me as a courageous, dangerous man, one might say. . . . Well, yes . . . But now, just recently, something came upon me . . . the evil eye, you know. A frailty. One week ago. I'm sitting by a lamp, you know, and suddenly a question comes to mind: why, thus far, hasn't your foot slipped? And what if it slips tomorrow and you're in trouble?"

"Surely you must have thought this many times."

"Of course! Many times! But this time it wasn't the end of it—because right away another thought came to mind, that I shouldn't think this way because it may, should the occasion arise, soften me, leave me wide open, devil only knows, lay me bare to danger. I figured I had better not think that way. But, as soon as I thought that, I couldn't chase the thought away, it just caught me, and now I'm constantly, constantly thinking that my foot will slip, and so it goes in circles. Listen! It caught me!"

"Nerves."

"It's not nerves. You know what it is? It's a transformation. A transformation of courage into fear. It can't be helped."

He lit a cigarette. He inhaled, blew out the match.

"Imagine, only three weeks ago I had a goal ahead of me, a task, I had a battle ahead, some object or other. . . . Now I have nothing. Everything fell away from me, my pants are down, if you'll excuse the expression. Now my only thought is that nothing should happen to me. And I'm right. Whoever fears for himself is always right! The worst of it is that I'm right, not until now have I been right! And what do you all want from me? This is my fifth day here. I ask for horses—they won't give them to me. You're holding me like a prisoner. What do you all want to do with me? I'm writhing in that little room upstairs. . . . What is it you want?"

"Calm down. It's all nerves."

"You want to finish me off?"

"You're exaggerating."

"I'm not so stupid. I've let people down. . . . Unfortunately I blabbed about my fear, now they know. As long as I wasn't afraid of them they feared me. Now that I'm scared, I've become dangerous. I understand that. I can't be trusted. But I'm turning to you, as a human being. I made the following decision: to get up, come to you, and speak directly. This is my last chance. I come to you directly because someone in my situation has no other choice. Please hear me, it's a vicious circle. You're all afraid of me because I'm afraid of you, I'm afraid of you because you're afraid of me. I can't extricate myself from this except with a jump, and that's why, boom, I bang on your door at night, even though we don't know each other. . . . You're an intelligent man, a writer, so please understand me, offer me your hand, so that I can extricate myself from this."

"What can I do?"

"Get them to let me leave. Let me break loose. That's all I dream of. To break loose. Back out. I'd leave on foot—except that you're likely to nab me in the fields somewhere and . . . Please persuade them to let me go, convince them that I won't hurt anyone, that I'm fed up, that I can't stand it any more. I want to be—at peace. At peace. Once we separate, there will be no difficulties. Please, sir, do it for me, I implore you, because, you know, I can't . . . Help me escape. I'm turning to you because I can't be all alone against everyone else, like an outlaw, lend me your hand, don't leave me like this. We don't know each other, but I've chosen you. I've come to you. Why do you all want to persecute me now that I've become totally harmless—completely so! It's all done with."

This was an unexpected hitch in the shape of this man who started shaking. . . . what was I to tell him? I was still full of

Vaclav, and here, in front of me, this man is spewing—enough, enough, enough!—and asking for mercy. In a flash I saw the total disaster of the problem: I couldn't turn him away because now his death was intensified by the life trembling in front of me. He had come to me, he became close and hence enormous, his life and death were now mounting in front of me, sky high. At the same time his arrival returned me—by wresting me from Vaclav—to duty, to our action under Hipolit's leadership, and he, Siemian, was becoming merely the object of our activity . . . and, as an object, he was thrown outside us, excluded from us, and I couldn't acknowledge him, or communicate with him, or really talk with him, I had to keep my distance and, by not letting him close to me, I had to maneuver, play politics . . . and so my spirit stood on its hind legs like a horse before an insurmountable obstacle . . . because he was calling upon my humanity and getting close to me as a human being, while I wasn't permitted to see him as a human being. What kind of answer should I give him? The most important thing was—not to let him get close to me, not to let him sink into me! "Sir," I said, "there is a war on. The country is under occupation. Desertion under these conditions is a luxury we cannot afford. We have to watch one another. You know that."

"This means . . . you don't really want . . . to talk with me?"

He waited a moment, as if savoring the silence that was separating us more and more. "Sir," he said, "haven't you ever been caught with your pants down?"

Again I didn't answer, increasing the distance. "Sir," he said patiently, "Everything fell away from me—I have nothing. Let's talk without further ado. Since I'm coming to you by night, as a stranger to a stranger, let's talk and skip the rest, shall we?"

He fell silent and waited for me to say something. I said nothing.

"No matter what your opinion of me is," he added with apathy. "I chose you—as my savior or my killer. Which do you prefer?"

I then handed him an obvious lie—as obvious to me as it was to him—and thus I finally threw him out of our circle: "I know nothing about any threats against you. You're exaggerating. It's nerves."

This floored him. He said nothing—he didn't move, he didn't leave, he just remained . . . passive. It was as if I had deprived him of the ability to leave. And I thought this could go on for hours, he won't move, why should he move—he'll stay here . . . and keep weighing me down. I didn't know what to do with him—and he couldn't help me because I had rejected him, thrown him out, and without him I found myself with regard to him—alone . . . as if I were holding him in my hand. And between me and him there was nothing but indifference, cold unfriendliness, revulsion, he was a stranger to me, he was disgusting! A dog, a horse, a hen, even a bug were more pleasing to me than this man, in his years, worn out, his whole history written all over him—a grown man can't stand another grown man! There is nothing more repulsive to a grown man than another grown man—I'm talking, of course, about older men, their history written on their faces. He was not attractive to me, no! He was incapable of winning me over. He was unable to put himself into my graces. Unable to please me! His spiritual being was as repulsive to me as his carnal being, just like Vaclav's, even more so—I was repulsive to him, just as he was repulsive to me, we would have locked horns like two old aurochs—and the fact that I, in my wasted state, was equally disgusting to him intensified my disgust for him even further. Vaclav—and now he—both hideous! And I with them! A grown man can be bearable to another grown man only in the form of self-denial, when he denies himself for the sake of something—honor, virtue, nation, struggle. . . . But a grown man merely as a grown man—what a monstrosity!

Yet he chose me. He presented himself to me—and now he was not giving in. He was here in front of me. I coughed, and this little cough made me aware that the situation was becoming more and more difficult. His death—even though revolting—was now only a step away from me, like something that could not be avoided.

I was dreaming of only one thing—that he would leave. I'll think about it later, let him leave first. Why shouldn't I say that I agree with him and will help him? It wasn't binding, I could, after all, turn this promise into a ruse and a maneuver—if I were to decide to destroy him, that is, and reveal everything to

Hipolit—actually, this would be advisable, for the sake of the goals of our activity, our group, to secure his confidence and to manipulate him. If I decide to destroy him . . . then what's the harm in lying to a man whom one is destroying?

"Listen, please. First of all—control your nerves. This is the most important thing. Come down to lunch tomorrow. Say that you had a nervous crisis and it's now passing. That you are returning to form. Pretend you're all right. For my part, I'll also talk to Hipolit and try somehow to arrange your departure. Now go back to your room, someone could come here. . . ."

I had no idea what I was saying. Truth or lie? Help or treason? It will become clear later—but now let him go away! He rose and drew himself up. I didn't notice any trace of hope, not a muscle twitched, he tried neither to thank me nor to please me, not even by his gaze . . . because he knew in advance that nothing would succeed, that there was nothing left for him except to be, to be as he is, to be his own awkward being, his unpleasant self—whose destruction, however, would be even more disgusting. He was merely blackmailing me with his existence. . . . Oh, how different this was from Karol!

Karol!

After Siemian's departure I began writing a letter to Fryderyk. It was a report—I reported on both these nocturnal visits. And this was the document by which I was clearly presenting myself to our joint activity. I was presenting myself in writing. I began a dialogue.

XI

Next day Siemian appeared at lunch.

I rose late and came down just as everyone was coming to the table—and then Siemian appeared, shaved, pomaded, and perfumed, a handkerchief sticking out of his breast pocket. This was the arrival of a corpse—we had been, after all, in the process of putting him to death for two days running, without a break. The corpse, however, kissed Madame Maria's hand with the grace of a cavalryman and, having greeted everyone, explained that "the indisposition that had overcome him was beginning to pass," that he was feeling better—that he was fed up with stewing by himself upstairs while "the whole family was gathered here." Hipolit himself moved a chair toward him, his place setting was quickly arranged, our attention to him returned as if it had never changed, he sat down—as overpowering and overbearing as he had been that first evening. Soup was served. He asked for vodka. This must have been no trifling effort—corpse talking, corpse eating, corpse drinking, an effort violently wrested from his all-powerful disinclination, wrested merely by the power of fear. "My appetite isn't the best yet, but I'll try a little soup." "A swig of vodka, if you please."

The lunch . . . miserable yet marked by hidden dynamics, abounding in exuberant crescendos and imbued with contradictory meanings, blurry, like a text written within another text . . . Vaclav at his place next to Henia—he must have had a talk with her and "won her over with his respect," because they both showed a great deal of attention to each other, now and again exchanging pleasantries, she became more refined and he became more refined—they both became more refined. As far as Fryderyk was concerned—loquacious as always, sociable, but obviously pushed into the background by Siemian, who imperceptibly took the reins. . . . Yes, even more than when he first appeared, there was a contagion of obedience and inner tension with regard to his wishes, the tiniest ones, which began with him as a request and ended with us as commands. Since I already knew that it was wretchedness dressed up, out of fear, in his former, now lost, imperiousness, I saw this as a farce! At first it was masked as the good-heartedness of an East Poland officer, a bit Cossack-like, a bit swashbuckling—yet gloom began to ooze from all his pores, gloom, as well as the cold, apathetic indifference that I had noticed yesterday. He was turning dark and ugly. And this entanglement, taking place within him, must have been unbearable to him, while before our eyes and out of fear, he was taking shape as the old Siemian he no longer was, whom he feared more than we did, whom he could no longer match—the old, the "dangerous" Siemian, who was the one to give commands and use people, the one to order one man to put another man to death. "I'd like to ask you for a slice of lemon"—it sounded so good-natured, charmingly East Poland, even somewhat in the old Russian style, but it had claws, somewhere deep down it was marked by disrespect for the existence of others, and he, sensing it, was frightened, and his terror fed on his fear. Fryderyk, I knew, must have been soaking up this simultaneous accumulation of terror and fear rolled into one. Yet Siemian's game would not have become so unrestrained if Karol had not teamed up with him from the other end of the table, supporting Siemian's imperiousness with his whole being.

Karol was eating soup, buttering bread—yet Siemian immediately took control of him just as he had done at their first encounter. Again the boy had a lord over him. His hands became soldier-like and dexterous. His whole undeveloped existence instantly and smoothly surrendered to Siemian, surrendered and submitted to him—when Karol ate it was to serve him, he buttered his bread with Siemian's permission, and his head promptly submitted itself to him with its short-cut hair swirling softly on his forehead. He was not expressing it in some manner—he simply became it, like someone who changes with the lighting. It's possible that Siemian wasn't aware of it, nonetheless, a relationship was soon cemented between himself and the boy, and Siemian's gloom, that unfriendly cloud loaded with imperiousness (now only feigned) began to seek out Karol and pile itself upon him. And Vaclav helped it along, Vaclav the refined, sitting next to Henia . . . Vaclav the just, demanding love and virtue . . . watched the chief made dark by the boy, the boy—by the chief.

He must have sensed it—Vaclav—that this was turning against the very respect which he had been defending and which was defending him—because between the chief and the boy there was evolving none other than actual disdain—disdain first and foremost for death. Wasn't the boy giving himself to the chief, life and death, exactly because the other was afraid neither to die nor to kill—this is what gave him sovereignty over others. And in the wake of such disdain for death and life came other possible debasements, whole oceans of devaluations, and the boy's ability for disdain bonded with the man's gloomy, imperious nonchalance—they acknowledged one another, for they were not afraid of death or pain, one because he was a boy, the other because he was the chief. The matter sharpened and grew because phenomena elicited artificially are more unbridled—since, after all, Siemian was making himself a chief simply out of fear, to rescue himself. And this artificial chief, whom the young one was changing into reality, was strangling him, choking him, terrorizing him. Fryderyk must have been soaking up (I knew) the sudden gain in power by the other three, Siemian's, Karol's and Vaclav's, heralding the possibility of an explosion . . . while she, Henia, was calmly bending over her plate.

Siemian was eating . . . to show that he was now able to eat like everyone else . . . and he tried to charm with his charm from the steppes, a charm which was, however, poisoned by his corpse-like chill and which, in Karol, was immediately transforming itself into violence and into blood. Fryderyk was soaking this up. But then it so happened that Karol asked for a glass and Henia handed it to him—and perhaps that moment, when the glass went from one hand to the other hand, was a little, only slightly, prolonged, it seemed that she was late by a fraction of a second in withdrawing her hand. It could be so. Was it? This trifle of evidence reached Vaclav like a bludgeon—he turned gray—while Fryderyk brushed them with his oh so indifferent gaze.

Compote was served. Siemian fell silent. Now he sat, increasingly unpleasant, as if he had run out of politeness, and he seemed to have finally given up on pleasing, as if the gates of horror had opened wide before him. He was frigid. Henia began to play with her fork, and it so happened that Karol was also touching his fork—actually it wasn't clear whether he was playing with it or just touching it, it could be pure happenstance, indeed the fork was close at hand—nonetheless Vaclav again turned gray—was it indeed happenstance? Oh, of course, it could have been happenstance—so trivial it was almost imperceptible. Yet it was conceivable . . . what if this trifle was actually giving them permission for a prank, oh so slight, so lightweight, so microscopic that (the girl) could be submitting to it with (the boy) while not violating her virtue with regard to her fiancé—indeed, it was all totally imperceptible. . . . And wasn't it this very lightness that was tempting them—since the lightest movement of their hands hit Vaclav like a blow—perhaps they couldn't restrain themselves from their little amusement that, being almost nothing, was at the same time—for Vaclav—a crushing defeat. Siemian finished eating his compote. Even if Karol really was teasing Vaclav, oh, perhaps imperceptibly even to himself, this in no way violated his fidelity toward Siemian, since he was amusing himself like a soldier, ready for death and therefore behaving recklessly. And this too was marked by the strangely unbridled behavior that artificiality bestows—since the little game with the forks was, after all, merely a sequel to the theater on the island, the flirting between them was "theatrical." I thus found myself, at this table, between two perplexities, more intense than anything reality could muster. An artificial chief and an artificial love.

Everyone rose. Lunch had come to an end.

Siemian stepped up to Karol.

"Hey you . . . kid. . . ," he said.

"What's up?!" Karol replied, delighted.

Then the officer turned his pale eyes to Hipolit, coldly, unpleasantly. "Shall we talk?" he suggested through his teeth.

I wanted to be present at their conversation but he stopped me with a curt: "You—no. . . ." What was this? A command? Had he forgotten how we talked last night? But I complied with his wish and stayed on the verandah, while he and Hipolit walked away into the garden. Henia was next to Vaclav and placed her hand on his shoulder as if nothing had taken place between them, faithful again, but Karol, standing at the open door, didn't fail to place his hand on it (his hand on the door—her hand on Vaclav). And the fiancé said to the young girl: "Let's go for a walk." To which she replied like an echo: "Let's go." They went away down the lane, while Karol was left behind like an unrestrained joke that nobody could get. . . . Fryderyk muttered, "This is ridiculous!" as he watched the betrothed couple and Karol. My imperceptible smile answered him . . . for him alone.

After a quarter of an hour Hipolit returned and summoned us to his study.

"We have to get rid of him," he said. "The job has to be done tonight. He's pressuring us!"

And, dropping to the couch, he repeated to himself with pleasure, lowering his eyes: "He's pressuring us!"

It turned out that Siemian had again demanded horses—but this time it was not a request—no, it was something that made Hipolit unable to regain his balance for quite a while. "Gentlemen, he's a scoundrel! He's a murderer! He wanted horses, I said I didn't have them today, maybe tomorrow . . . then he squeezed my hand with his fingers, he took my hand in his fingers and squeezed it, I tell you, like a typical killer . . . and he said that if by ten tomorrow morning the horses weren't there, then . . .

"He pressured me!" he said, terrified. "The job must be done tonight, because tomorrow *I will have to* give him horses."

And he added softly:

"I will have to."

This was a surprise to me. Apparently Siemian couldn't sustain the role we had planned yesterday, and instead of talking cordially, soothingly, he was threatening. . . . It was clear he had been invaded, terrorized, by the ex-Siemian, the dangerous one that he had called up during lunch, and this created a threat within him, a command, pressure, cruelty (which he couldn't resist, since he was more afraid of these than anyone else). . . . Suffice it to say, he again became a threat. At least it was good that I no longer felt solely responsible for him, as I had felt last night, in my room, since I had passed this matter on to Fryderyk.

Hipolit rose. "Gentlemen, well, how shall we do it? And who?" He pulled out four matches and twisted the little head off one of them. I looked at Fryderyk—I waited for a sign—should I reveal my nocturnal conversation with Siemian? But I saw that he was terribly pale. He swallowed saliva.

"Excuse me," he said, "I don't know whether . . ."

"What?" Hipolit asked.

"Death," Fryderyk said briefly. He was looking aside. "To k-i-l-l him?"

"What else? These are the orders."

"To k-i-l-l," he repeated. He wasn't looking at anyone. He was tête-à-tête with this word. There was no one else—just he and to k-i-l-l. His chalk-white paleness couldn't lie, it came from the fact that *he knew what it was to kill.* He knew it—at this moment—to the very depths. "I . . . will not . . . this . . . ," he said and shook his fingers somehow sideways, sideways, sideways, somewhere behind him. . . . All of a sudden he turned his face toward Vaclav.

It was as if a suggestion of something appeared on his paleness—before he even spoke I knew with certainty that he had not broken down but was continuing to direct events, that he was maneuvering—not letting Henia and Karol out of his sight—in their direction! What then? Was he scared? Or was he chasing them?

"Not you either!" he turned directly to Vaclav.

"Not me?"

"How could you do it . . . with a knife—because it must be done with a knife, not with a revolver, that's too loud—how could you do it with a knife when just recently your mother was . . . also with a knife? You? You and your mother, and a Catholic too? I ask you! How could you possibly manage to do it?"

He was becoming tangled in words, but they had been thoroughly lived through, supported by his face that, while shouting "no," was glued to Vaclav's face. Undoubtedly—"he knew what he was talking about." He knew what it meant "to kill," and he was at the end of his endurance, and unequal to the task. . . . No, this was not a game, nor tactics, at this moment he was genuine!

"Are you a deserter?" Hipolit asked coldly.

In reply Fryderyk smiled helplessly and stupidly.

Vaclav swallowed saliva as if he had been forced to eat something inedible. I think that up to now he had been approaching this just as I was, that is, in the mode of war, that this killing was for him one of many, one more killing—repulsive yet after all ordinary and even necessary, and unavoidable—but now it was extracted for him out of many and placed separately, as something immense. Killing as such! He too went pale. After all, his mother! And the knife! A knife identical to the one that his mother . . . He would in this case be killing with a knife that had been pulled out of his mother, he would be aiming with the same thrust and would be repeating the same act on Siemian's body. . . . Yet it was possible that behind his tensely wrinkled brow his mother became mixed up with Henia, and it was not his mother but actually Henia who became the deciding factor. He must have perceived himself in Skuziak's role, administering the blow . . . but then, how was he to endure Henia with Karol, how could he resist their coupling, resist Henia in the (boy's) embrace, the not yet matured Henia in his arms, Henia brazenly beboyed? . . . To kill Siemian just as Skuziak had done—but who would he then become? Another Skuziak? But what would then counter that other force—the juvenile one? Had Fryderyk not isolated and overblown the Kill . . . but now it would be a Kill, and this blow with the knife would strike at his very dignity, his honor, virtue, everything he had used to fight against Skuziak for his mother, against Karol for Henia.

This was probably why, turning to Hipolit, he announced bluntly, as if stating something already known:

"I can't do it. . . ."

Fryderyk said to me, almost triumphantly, with a tone that demanded a reply:

"And you? Will you kill him?"

Ha! What? So this was merely a tactic! He was driving at something while feigning fear, forcing us to refuse. Inconceivable: this fear of his, pale, sweating, trembling, so extreme, was merely a horse on which he was galloping . . . to the young knees and hands! He was using his dread for erotic ends! A pinnacle of fraud, unbelievable baseness, something unacceptable and unbearable! He treated himself as he did his horse! But his onward rush seized me, and I felt I had to gallop with him. And, clearly, I did not want to kill. I was happy that I was allowed to squirm out of it—our discipline and unity had already cracked. I replied: "No."

"What a mess," Hipolit rejoined coarsely. "Enough of this baloney. In that case I'll do the job myself. Without anyone's help."

"You?" asked Fryderyk. "You?"

"I."

"No."

"Why?"

"Nnno . . ."

"Listen," Hipolit said, "just think of it. One can't be a swine. One needs to have some sense of duty. This is duty, sir! This is military service!"

"You want, out of a sense of duty, to k-i-l-l an innocent man?"

"These are the orders. We received orders. This is war, sir! I will not break ranks, we must all stand together. We must! It's our responsibility! What do you want? To let him go alive?"

"Impossible," Fryderyk agreed. "I know that's impossible."

Hipolit stared at us. Did he expect Fryderyk to say: "Yes, let him go?" Was he counting on it? If that was his secret hope, Fryderyk's reply had cut off the retreat.

"So what do you want?"

"I know, of course . . . necessity . . . duty . . . orders . . . One cannot not . . . But you won't . . . You will not slaugh-ter him. . . . You will nnnot. . . . You can't!"

Hipolit, coming up against that modest, softly spoken "nno"—sat down. That "nno" knew what it meant to kill—and this knowledge, at this moment, was directing itself at him, piling up enormous difficulties. Encased in his large body he looked at us as if through a window, his eyes staring out. An "ordinary" liquidation of Siemian was no longer an option after our three refusals, full of repugnance. Under the pressure of our revulsion, it became disgusting. And he could no longer allow himself to be shallow. Although he was not a deep or shrewd person, he was a man of a certain circle, a certain class, and as we had become deep he could not remain shallow, if only for social reasons. In certain instances one cannot be "less deep," just as one cannot be "less refined", being so disqualifies one socially. And this is how convention forced him to be deep, to exhaust, in unison with us, the meaning of the word "kill", he saw it, as we saw it—as an atrocity. He suddenly felt, as we did, helpless. To murder someone with one's own hands? No, no, no! But in that case all that was left was "not to kill"—but "not to kill" actually meant to break away, to betray, to be a coward, not to fulfill one's obligation! He spread his hands. He was between two abominations—and one of them must become his abomination.

"What then?" he asked.

"Let Karol deal with it."

Karol! So this is what Fryderyk was driving at all along—that fox! The slyboots! Mounting himself, as if mounting a horse!

"Karol?"

"Sure. He'll do the job. If you order him."

He said it as if it were incredibly easy—for him the difficulty had vanished. As if it meant Karol shopping in Ostrowiec. It wasn't clear why this change in tone seemed somehow justified. Hipolit wavered.

"We should put it on him?"

"Who else? We won't do it, this isn't our sort of thing . . . yet it needs to be done, it can't be helped! You'll tell him. He'll do it if he's told. It won't be a problem for him. Why shouldn't he do it? Order him."

"Of course, if I order him he'll do it. . . . But how's that? What? So he's supposed to . . . instead of us?"

Vaclav anxiously intervened.

"You're not taking into account that it's risky. . . . It's a responsibility. One can't just use him, shift the risk to him. That's impossible! It's not done!"

"We can take the risk upon ourselves. If the matter comes to light we'll say that we are the perpetrators. What's the problem? It's only a matter of someone else taking the knife and slashing him—it'll go more smoothly for him than for us."

"But I'm telling you that we have no right to use him just because he's sixteen years old, shove him into this . . . have him do our work. . . ."

He was panicking. To shove Karol into a murder that he himself wasn't capable of committing, taking advantage of Karol's youth. Karol—just because he's a kid . . . this was indeed not right, and it weakened him in relation to the boy . . . even as he had to be strong in relation to the boy! He began to pace the room. "It would be immoral!" he exploded in anger and blushed like someone whose most callous shame had been touched. Hipolit, however, was slowly getting used to the idea.

"It's feasible . . . the simplest thing really. . . . No one is shirking responsibility. It's only a matter of not getting oneself dirty . . . with the act itself. . . . It's not a job for us. It's just right for him."

And he calmed down as if touched by a magician's wand—as if the only natural solution had finally presented itself. He realized this was something in keeping with nature's order. He wasn't shirking. He was the one to give orders—and Karol the one to carry them out.

He regained his calm and his wisdom. He became aristocratic.

"It hadn't occurred to me. But of course!"

A rather remarkable sight indeed: two men, one man shamed by something that returned dignity to the other. The "taking advantage of a juvenile" filled one of them with a feeling of disgrace, the other with pride—and, as a result, it was as if it made one less masculine, the other more masculine. Yet Fryderyk was—oh, so brilliant! To be able to involve Karol in this . . . twisting the whole business toward him . . . and thanks to that the intended death heated up at once and flared up, not only due to Karol but also due to Henia, their hands, legs—and the planned corpse suddenly bloomed with the forbidden, boy-girl, awkward, coarse sensuality. Heat has made an ingress—the death now became amatory. And everything—the death, our fear, repugnance, helplessness—was there merely so that a young hand, too young, would reach for it. . . . I was already becoming immersed in it, not as if it were a murder, but as an escapade of their underdeveloped, dumb bodies. What a delight!

And at the same time there was malicious irony, even a taste of defeat—that we, grownups, were resorting to the help of a youngster who could do what we couldn't do—was this murder a cherry on a thin branch, accessible only to someone lighter? . . . Lightness! All of a sudden everything began to press in that direction, Fryderyk, myself, Hipolit, we all began to make our way toward the juvenile, as if by a secret alchemy that was easing our burden.

Suddenly Vaclav also gave his consent to use Karol.

Had he refused, he would be the one to deal with it, since we were already out of the contest. And second, he must have become confused—his Catholicism must have raised its voice, and all of a sudden he must have imagined that Karol, as a murderer, would become as abhorrent to Henia as he, Vaclav, as a murderer—a mistake that originated from the fact that he was smelling the flowers with his soul rather than with his nose, he believed too strongly in the beauty of virtue and in the ugliness of sin. He forgot that crime might take on a different flavor in Karol than in him. Latching on to that illusion, he agreed—because he actually couldn't disagree if he didn't want to break with us and find himself, in these dubious circumstances, totally by the wayside.

Fryderyk, fearing they might change their minds, immediately began to look for Karol—and I went with him. He was not in the house. We saw Henia taking the laundry from a dresser, but she was not the one we needed. Our nervousness increased. Where was Karol? We were looking for him with increasing haste, not talking, as if we were strangers.

He was in the stable, attending to the horses—we called him out—he came up to us, smiling. I remember that smile well, because the moment we called him I realized how reckless our proposal was. He adored Siemian, after all. He was devoted to him. How could one force him to do such a thing? But his smile instantly carried us into a different realm, where everything was friendly and eager. This child was already aware of his advantages. He knew that if there was anything we wanted from him it was his youth—so he approached us, scoffing slightly, but also ready to have fun. And his approach was filled with happiness, because it showed how chummy he had become with us. And it was a strange thing: the fun, the smiling lightness, was the best introduction to the brutality that was about to take place.

"Siemian has turned traitor," Fryderyk clarified succinctly. "There is evidence."

"Aha!" Karol said.

"He must be bumped off today, tonight. Will you do it?"

"Me?"

"Are you afraid?"

"No."

He stood by the whiffletree on which the harness was hanging. Nothing whatsoever hinted at his fidelity to Siemian. As soon as he heard about the killing he turned taciturn, perhaps even a bit embarrassed. He closed up and stiffened. It seemed he wouldn't object. I realized that to kill Siemian, or to kill on Siemian's orders, was one and the same thing to him—what united him with Siemian was death, no matter whose. In relation to Siemian he was blindly obedient and a soldier—but he was also obedient and a soldier when he was turning against Siemian on our orders. It was apparent that his blind obedience to the chief turned into an instantaneous, silent ability to put someone to death. It didn't surprise him.

It's just that (the boy) looked at us briefly. His look held a secret (as if he were asking: are you after Siemian or . . . after me?). But he said nothing. He became circumspect.

Overwhelmed by this incredible easiness (that seemed to take us into an entirely different dimension) we went with him to Hipolit, who gave him additional instructions—that he needs to go at night with a knife—that everything is to take place without noise. Hipolit had already totally regained his balance and was giving instructions like an officer—he was at his station.

"And what if he doesn't open the door? Surely he locks himself in."

"We'll find a way to get him to open it."

Karol left.

And the fact that he left agitated and infuriated me. Where did he go? To his room? What did this mean—his room? What was this, this realm of his, where one dies as easily as one kills? We came upon a readiness, an obedience that indicated how well-suited he was for this—that's how smoothly it went! Oh, he left us so beautifully, quietly, obediently . . . and I had no doubt that he went to her, to Henia, with those hands where we had placed a knife. Henia! There was no doubt that now, as a boy with a knife, a boy putting someone to death, he was closer to conquering and possessing her—were it not for Hipolit, who stopped us for further counsel, we would have run after him to spy. But after a while we left Hipolit's study in order to go into the garden, to follow him, her—and no sooner had we reached the hallway than we heard Vaclav's muffled voice, suddenly cut short, coming from the dining room—something had happened there! We went in. The scene was like one of those on the island. Vaclav was two steps from Henia—we didn't know what their problem was, but something must have happened between them.

Karol was standing a little farther away, by the sideboard.

When he saw us, Vaclav said:

"I slapped her face."

He left.

She then said:

"He's hitting me!"

"He's hitting her," Karol repeated.

They were laughing. Snickering. Maliciously yet amused. Not really—not overly—they were just snickering a bit. What elegance in their snickering! And they rather enjoyed his "hitting" her, they seemed to get off on it.

"What's come over him?" Fryderyk asked. "What upset him?"

"What do you think?" she asked. She cast a glance with amusement, coquettishly, and we understood at once that this had to do with Karol. It was so wonderful, so charming, that she didn't even indicate him with her eyes, she knew it wasn't necessary—she had become coquettish, and that was enough—

she knew we would like her only "with" Karol. How easily we could now communicate—and I saw that they were both sure of our goodwill. Playful, frolicking discreetly, perfectly cognizant that they were ravishing us. This was obvious.

It wasn't difficult to guess that Vaclav couldn't stand it—they must have teased him again with an almost imperceptible look or touch . . . oh, those childish provocations of theirs! Fryderyk asked her abruptly:

"Did Karol tell you anything?"

"About what?"

"About tonight . . . what he'll do . . . to Siemian . . ."

He made a funny gesture imitating cutting a throat—it would have been funny if the fun were not something so serious. He was having fun, in all seriousness. He sat down. No, she knew nothing, Karol hadn't let her in on anything. So Fryderyk briefly told her about the planned "liquidation," and that Karol was to carry it out. He talked about it as if it pertained to something totally ordinary. They (since Karol was still here) listened—how shall I put it—without opposing it. They couldn't listen in any other way, because they had to please us, and this made it difficult for them to react. The significant thing was that when he finished she said not a word—nor did he—and their silence grew. It wasn't exactly clear what it meant. But (the boy), there, by the sideboard, stood gloomy, and she too turned dark.

Fryderyk went on to explain: "The main difficulty is that at night Siemian may not open the door. He'll be afraid. You could both go together. You, Henia, could knock on the door under some pretext. He will open it for you. It won't even dawn on him not to open it. You'll say, for example, that you have a letter for him. And when he opens the door, you'll step back and Karol will slide in . . . this seems the best way . . . what do you both think?"

He was suggesting this without undue pressure, "just so," which made sense—because the whole plan was already stretching it, there was no assurance that Siemian would open the door for her just like that, Fryderyk was barely hiding the real meaning behind this suggestion: to pull Henia into it, so that they would both . . . He was setting it up like the scene on the island. It wasn't just the idea that dazzled me, but rather the way it was carried into life—because he was suggesting it out of the blue, almost casually, and he took advantage of the moment when they were particularly inclined to treat us graciously, to be our allies, or to simply charm us—both together, both together! It was obvious that Fryderyk was counting on the couple's "goodwill"—that they would agree without great difficulty in order to satisfy him—he was thus counting again on the "ease," the same ease that Karol had already demonstrated. He simply wanted them to crush the worm "together." . . . But now the erotic, sensual, love-like meaning of his design was barely hidden—it was obvious! And I thought for a moment that the two faces of this venture were struggling with each other right in front of us: because on the one hand the proposal was rather horrible, since it surely meant also sticking the girl into sin, into murder . . . but on the other hand the proposal was "intoxicating and exciting," because the purpose was for them to be in it "together." . . .

Which will prevail? I had enough time for the question to run through my head, since they didn't reply straight off. At the same time I saw clearly that, as they stood here before us, they continued to be unfriendly *toward each other*, without tenderness, harsh—and yet in spite of it they were so pinned down by the fact that they were ravishing us and that we expected to be intoxicated by them, that they were forced into submission. They could no longer go against the beauty we were discovering in them. And, deep down, this submission suited them—they were, after all, meant to submit. This was again one of those acts "done unto oneself," so typical of youth, acts which define youth and which therefore intoxicate youth to such a degree that they almost lose their objective, external meaning. Not Siemian, not his death, was to them paramount—only themselves. (The girl) limited herself to replying:

"Why not? It can be done."

Karol suddenly laughed a silly laugh.

"If it can be done, it will be done, if it can't be done, it won't be done."

I sensed that he needed this silliness.

"Well, then. You'll knock on the door, then get out of the way and I'll bump him off. That's how it'll be, but we don't know if he'll open the door."

She laughed. "Don't worry, if I knock he'll open."

She was being rather silly herself now.

"Of course this is just between us," Fryderyk said. "Don't worry!"

The conversation ended here—such conversations shouldn't be prolonged. I walked onto the verandah, from there into the garden. I wanted to breathe—everything was rushing on too swiftly. Light was waning. Colors lost the shine of their glassy coating, the greens and reds ceased to sting—a shadow-like relaxation of hues before nightfall. What does night conceal? Namely . . . the crushing of the worm—Siemian was the worm, not Vaclav. I wasn't sure the whole thing hung together, a murky fire warmed and ignited me every now and then, yet I repeatedly grew disheartened, discouraged, even despairing, because it was all too fantastic, too unrestrained, too unreal—frolicking, yes, but on our part it was actually "playing with fire." Finding myself all by myself, among shrubs, I totally lost the thread. . . . I suddenly saw Vaclav approaching. "I want to explain things to you! Please understand me! I wouldn't have hit her, but it was swinish, I tell you, simply swinish!"

"What was?"

"It was swinish of her! Totally swinish, thinly veiled, but still . . . and it was not my imagination. . . . Thinly veiled swinishness, yet coarse! We were talking in the dining room. Enter—he. The lover. I sensed at once that she was talking to me but addressing him."

"Addressing him?"

"Him, not with words but . . . with everything else. All of her. She seemed to be talking to me, yet at the same time she was accosting him and giving herself to him. In my presence. While talking to me. Would you believe it? It was something . . . I saw that she was talking to me while she was with him—and with him so . . . totally. As if I wasn't even there. I hit her in the face. And now what am I to do? Tell me, what can I do now?"

"Can't it be smoothed over?"

"But I hit her! Period. I hit her! Now everything is definitely settled and finalized. I hit her! I don't know how I could have . . . Do you know what I think? If I had not let him be assigned to this . . . liquidation . . . I wouldn't have hit her."

"Why not?"

He looked at me sharply.

"Because I'm no longer in the right—with regard to him. I let him do my work for me. I lost my moral ground, that's why I hit her. I hit her because my suffering no longer has any meaning. It's not worthy of respect. It has lost its honor. That's why I hit, hit, hit. . . . I wouldn't just hit him—I'd kill him!"

"What are you saying!?"

"I would kill him with no trouble at all. . . . That's nothing! To kill . . . such a? Just like crushing a bug! A trifle! A trifle! Yet on the other hand killing such a . . . It's scandalous! And shameful! It's much harder than with a grown-up. It's impossible! Killing should take place only between grownups. But what if I cut her throat? . . . Just imagine! Don't worry. I'm only joking. These are all little jokes! They're making fun of me, so why shouldn't I joke around a bit! Great God, save me from this joke I've fallen into! O God, my God, you're my only succor! What was it I wanted to say? Ah yes, it's Siemian that I should kill . . . that's what I should do, there's still time, I must hurry . . . there's still time to take the murder away from this kid . . . because, as long as I'm using him I'm in the wrong, I'm in the wrong!"

He became lost in thought.

"It's too late. You've talked me into a corner. How can I take the task away from him now? Now it's obvious that I'm pushing myself into it not out of duty but merely not to give her to him—not to lose my moral advantage over her. All this morality of mine—merely to possess her!"

He spread his arms.

"I don't know what to do. I'm afraid there is nothing I can do."

He said a few more things worth noting:

"I'm naked! I feel so naked! My God! They've really stripped me! At my age I shouldn't be naked! Nudity is—for the young!"

And further:

"She's not only unfaithful to me. She's unfaithful to masculinity. Masculinity in general. Because she's unfaithful to me not with a grown man. Is she a woman then? No, I tell you, she's taking advantage of the fact that she's not yet a woman.

"They are taking advantage of some kind of separateness of theirs, something very pe-cu-liar, something that, until now, I never knew existed. . . ."

Further:

"But, I ask, how did it occur to them? I repeat what I've already said: they couldn't have contrived it by themselves. That thing on the island. What they are doing to me now . . . those provocations . . . It's too clever. I hope you understand me: they couldn't have thought it up, because it's too clever. So where did they get it? From books? I don't know!"

A thickening sauce was spilling below, obscuring vision, and though the crowns of trees were still basking in the feathery, cheerful sky, their trunks were already indistinct, pushing away one's gaze. I looked under the brick. A letter.

Please talk to Siemian.

Tell him that tonight you and Henia will escort him to the fields where Karol will be waiting with a britzka. Say that Henia will knock on his door tonight to escort him out. He'll believe it. He knows that Karol is his, and that Henia is Karol's! He'll believe it eagerly! This is the best way to get him to open the door when she knocks. This is important. Please do not fail to do it!

Please remember: there is no retreat. The only way to retreat is into swinishness.

Skuziak—what? What about him? I'm racking my brains. He can't be left out, all three of them should participate . . . but how?

Be careful! Don't force it. Better delicately and tactfully so as not to inflame the situation and risk failure needlessly, so far, knock on wood, luck has been on our side—it's all a matter of not ruining it. Take heed. Be careful!

I went to Siemian.

I knocked on his door—when he learned it was me, he opened the door, then immediately fell back onto his bed. How long had he been lying like that? In his socks—his boots, perfectly polished, were shining on the floor amid a pile of cigarette butts. He was smoking one cigarette after another. His hand, slim at the wrist, long, with a ring on his finger. He showed no inclination to talk. Lying supine, he watched the ceiling. I said I had come to warn him: have no illusions. Hipolit won't give him horses.

He didn't respond.

"Neither tomorrow, nor the day after. What's more, your concerns that they won't let you go alive are valid."

Silence.

"In which case I want to suggest to you . . . a plan of escape."

Silence.

"I want to help you."

He didn't respond.

He lay like a log. I thought he was afraid—but this was anger rather than fear. Spiteful anger. He lay and he was spitefully angry—nothing more. He was vicious. Because (I thought) I was privy to his weakness. I knew his weakness, that's why it had turned into anger.

I lay the plan before him. I alerted him that Henia would knock on his door, and that we would take him to the fields.

"Fuck it."

"Do you have any money?"

"I do."

"That's good. Be ready—a bit after midnight."

"Fuck it."

"This little expression won't help you much."

"Fuck it."

"Don't be so vulgar. We might lose interest."

"Fuck it."

I left him with that. He was accepting our help, letting us rescue him—but he wasn't thanking us. Having thrown himself on the bed, at full length, vigorous, he continued to present a predatory and authoritarian demeanor—the lord, the one in command—but he could no longer exert force on anything. His brute force had come to an end. And he knew that I knew it. Until recently he could threaten and impose power, he didn't need to ask anyone's favor, but now he was lying before me in his aggressive, furious masculinity that had been deprived of claws and was forced to seek sympathy . . . and he knew that he was unlikable, unpleasant, in this masculinity of his . . . and so he scratched his thigh with his stocking-clad foot . . . he lifted his leg and moved his toes, this was a perfectly egoistic gesture, he had had it up to his ass whether I liked him or not . . . he didn't like me . . . he was drowning in oceans of aversion, he wanted to puke . . . I did too. I left. His particular masculine cynicism was poisoning me, like cigarettes. In the dining room I came upon Hipolit and it threw me, I was a hair's breadth from vomiting, yes, a hair's breadth, one of those little hairs that grew on my hands and theirs! At this moment I couldn't stand the Grown Man!

There were—those men—five of them in the house. Hipolit, Siemian, Vaclav, Fryderyk, and I. Brrr . . . There is nothing in the animal kingdom that reaches such awfulness—is there a horse, a dog that can rival such looseness of form, such cynicism of form? Alas! Alas! After the age of thirty humanity steps into awfulness. *All beauty was on the other, the young, side.* I, a grown man, could not seek shelter among my colleagues, among grown men, because they were pushing me away. And they were pushing me into that other!

Madame Maria was standing on the verandah.

"Where is everybody?" she asked. "They've disappeared?"

"I don't know. . . . I was upstairs."

"And Henia? Did you see Henia?"

"Perhaps she's in the greenhouse."

She fluttered her fingers. "Don't you have the impression that . . . ? Vaclav seemed anxious to me. Despondent somehow. Is there something not quite right between them? Something seems to have gone wrong. I'm beginning to dislike this. I must have a chat with Vaclav . . . or perhaps with Henia. . . . I don't know. . . . O dear God!"

She was worried.

"I don't know anything. The fact that he's despondent . . . well, he lost his mother."

"Do you think that it's because of his mother?"

"Certainly. A mother is a mother!"

"You think so? I too think it's because of his mother. He lost his mother! Even Henia can't replace her! A mother is a mother! A mother!" She moved her fingers delicately. And this calmed her down completely, as if the word "mother" were so powerful that it took the meaning away even from the word "Henia," as if it were the highest sanctity! . . . Mother! Indeed, she too had been a mother. She had not actually been anything but a mother! Her former existence, having been exclusively a mother, looked at me with a withered, pluperfect gaze, it then withdrew, together with its veneration of mother—I knew there was no need to fear that she would thwart our plans—she, as a mother, wouldn't be able to affect anything at the present time. Her former, receding appeal came into play.

As night was approaching, along with whatever was announcing its arrival—the lighting of lamps, closing of shutters, setting the table for supper—I felt progressively worse, and I wandered about, unable to find a place for myself. The essence of my and Fryderyk's betrayal stood out with greater and greater sharpness: we had betrayed masculinity with (boy plus girl). Walking thus around the house I looked into the living room, where it was somewhat dark, and I saw Vaclav sitting on the couch. I went in and sat on an armchair, far from him, by the opposite wall. Muddied were my intentions. Fuzzy. A desperate test—to see if I could, with great effort, overcome my repugnance toward him and unite with him in masculinity. However, my repugnance has now grown sky high, aroused by my arrival and the placing of my body in the vicinity of his body—a repugnance awash with his animosity toward me . . . animosity that, making me disgusting, made my disgust toward him disgusting. And vice versa. I knew that under these conditions there was no question of either of us brightening up with that magnificence, which was, in spite of everything, accessible to us—I have in mind the magnificence of virtue, of wisdom, of sacrifice, of heroism that was embedded within us *in potentia*—but the disgust was all-powerful. Nonetheless, couldn't we overcome it with brute force? Brute force! Brute force! What were we men for? A man is someone who is aggressive, who overpowers by force. Man is the one who reigns! A man does not ask if anyone likes it, he cares only for his own pleasure, it's his taste that decides what is beautiful, what is ugly—for him, and for him alone! A man is just for himself, for no one else!

It was this aggressiveness that I was probably trying to kindle in us. . . . As far as matters stood at present, both he and I were impotent because we were not ourselves, nor were we there for each other, we were for the other, younger, way of feeling—and this was plunging us into ugliness. Yet, what if I had been able, in this living room, to be for him, for Vaclav, even for one moment—and he for me—what if we were able to be a man for a man! Wouldn't that have built up our masculinity? Wouldn't one man have forced his masculinity with masculinity on the other man? These were my calculations, created by what remained of my despairing and frantic hope. Because the brute force that is man must first be born of masculinity, between men . . . if only my mere presence with him could enclose us in a hermetic ring . . . I ascribed great meaning to the fact that darkness was further weakening what was already our Achilles' heel, namely our body. I thought that by taking advantage of the weakness of the body we would be able to unite and multiply, we would become men who were powerful enough so as not to be repulsive to ourselves—because, after all, no one is repulsive to oneself—because it's enough to be oneself in order not to be repulsive to oneself! These were my desperate enough intentions. But he remained motionless. . . . I did too. . . . We were unable to begin with each other, we lacked a beginning, we did not know how to begin. . . .

Suddenly Henia slipped into the living room.

She didn't notice me—she walked over to Vaclav—she sat

by him, quietly. As if—suggesting reconciliation. She was undoubtedly polite (I didn't see it clearly). Conciliatory. Affable. Meek. Helpless perhaps. Forlorn. What was this? What was this? Could she too have had enough . . . of that other stuff . . . was she scared, did she want to back out, looking for support from her fiancé, his help? She sat by him politely, without a word, leaving all the initiative to him, which meant: "You have me, so now do something with us." Vaclav didn't budge—he didn't move a finger.

Like a frog, motionless. I had no idea what raged within him. Pride? Jealousy? Umbrage? Or did he simply feel awkward not knowing what to do with her—while I wanted to scream, oh, that he would at least embrace her, place his hand on her, his salvation depended on it! The last resort! His hand on her would have regained masculinity, and I would have jumped to it with my hands, and everything would have somehow resolved itself! Brute force—brute force in the living room. Yet nothing. Time was passing. He didn't stir. And this was suicide—a flop—a flop—a flop—and the girl rose, walked away. . . and I followed her.

Supper was served, during which, because of Madame Maria, we turned to casual conversation. After supper I again didn't know what to do with myself, one would think that in the hours preceding a murder there would be a lot to do, yet not one of us did anything, everyone dispersed . . . perhaps because the deed that was to take place had such a secret, drastic character. Fryderyk? Where was Fryderyk? He too had disappeared, and his disappearance suddenly blinded me, as if a blindfold had been placed over my eyes, I didn't know what had happened, I had to find him, right now, right away—I began my search. I went outside. Rain was in the air, hot humidity, the wind rose at times and whirled about in the garden, then calmed down. I walked into the garden almost groping, guessing at the paths with a boldness that a step into the unseen necessitates, from time to time a familiar silhouette of a tree or a shrub announced that everything is as it should be, that I am where I expect to be. Yet I discovered that I was not at all prepared for the garden's immutability and that it rather surprised me. . . . I would have been less surprised if the garden had become topsy-turvy in the dark. This thought set me tossing about like a small boat on the open sea and I realized that I had already lost sight of land. Fryderyk wasn't there. I ventured as far as the islands, this venturing clouded my perception and every tree, every bush, crawling out in front of me became a fantasticality, attacking me—since even though they all were as they were, they *could have been* different. Fryderyk? Fryderyk? I needed him urgently. Without him everything was incomplete. Where was he hiding? What was he doing? I was returning to the house to look for him again when I happened upon him in the shrubs in front of the kitchen. He whistled like an urchin. He seemed displeased at my arrival, and even, possibly, somewhat embarrassed.

"What are you doing here?" I asked.

"I'm racking my brains."

"About what?"

"About this."

He pointed to the window of the pantry. At the same time he showed me something in his open hand. A key to the pantry. "Now we can talk," he said freely and in a full voice. "Letters are superfluous. She . . . you know . . . well . . . nature . . . she won't play tricks on us any more, because things have gone too far, the situation is clearly defined . . . No need to tiptoe! . . ." He was saying this in a strange way. Something peculiar radiated from him. Innocence? Sanctity? Purity? And, clearly, he had ceased to be afraid. He broke off a branch and threw it to the ground—at another time he would have wondered three times over whether to throw it or not to throw it. . . . "I brought this key with me," he added, "to force a solution on myself. As far as . . . that Skuziak is concerned."

"And so? Have you thought of something?"

"Indeed."

"May I ask what?"

"For the present . . . not yet . . . You'll see it at the appropriate moment. Or rather. I'll tell you now. Here you are."

He brought out his other hand—a knife in it, quite a large kitchen knife. "And what's this?" I asked, unpleasantly surprised. Suddenly and for the first time I realized with all certainty that I was dealing with a madman.

"I couldn't think of anything better," he confessed, as if justifying himself. "But this is enough. *Because if the young man kills the older man, then the older will kill the younger*—don't you see? This creates a whole. This will unite them, the three of them. The knife. I've known for a long time that what unites them is knife and blood. Of course, it must be carried out simultaneously," he added. "When Karol plunges his knife into Siemian, I'll plunge mine into Józaaa . . . aaak!"

What an idea! Crazy! Sick—insane—how can this be, he'll butcher him?! . . . And yet this insanity, somewhere, in some other dimension, was actually something quite natural, in and of itself understandable, this madman was right, it could be done, it would unite them, "unite into a whole." . . . The more bloody and horrible this absurdity, the more it united them. . . . And, as if this weren't enough, this sick idea, wafting as if from a hospital, degenerate and running wild, an intellectual's disgusting idea, exploded like a flowering shrub with a choking aroma, yes, it was delightful! It delighted me! Somewhere from the other side, from "their" side. This bloody enhancement of murderous youth and this uniting through a knife (of the boys with the girl). It was actually a matter of indifference what kind of cruelty was being perpetrated on them—or with them—any cruelty enhanced their flavor like hot sauce!

The invisible garden swelled and suffocated me with its charm—even though damp, even though gloomy, and with this monstrous madman around—I had to deeply breathe in its freshness, all of a sudden I was bathed in a wonderfully bitter, heartrendingly seductive elemental force. Everything, everything, everything became young and sensual again, even ourselves! And yet . . . no, I could not consent to this! He had definitely overstepped the bounds! This could not be tolerated—impossible—knifing this young fellow in the pantry—no, no, no . . . He broke into laughter.

"Oh, calm down! I just wanted to see if you have confidence that I don't have a screw loose. Really! Nothing of the sort! These are just daydreams . . . from sheer frustration that I haven't actually thought up anything with regard to this Skuziak. What an idiotic idea!"

An idiotic idea. Really. When he himself admitted it, the idiotic idea arrived in front of me as if on a platter, and I was displeased that I had fallen for it. We returned to the house.

XII

There is not much more to tell. Actually everything went smoothly, more and more smoothly, to an ending that . . . well, surpassed our expectations. And it was easy. . . . I felt like laughing that such a crushing difficulty was ending with such winged ease.

My role was again to watch Siemian's room. I lay on my bed, supine, hands under my head, straining my ears—we entered into night, the house was ostensibly asleep. I was waiting for the creaking of the steps under the feet of the killing little couple, but it was too early, by five minutes. Silence. Hipolit was standing guard in the courtyard. Fryderyk was downstairs, by the entrance. Finally, at twelve-thirty sharp the stairs creaked somewhere downstairs under their feet—shoes off most likely. Bare? Or in socks?

Unforgettable moments! A gentle creaking of the stairs became audible again. Why were they sneaking up like that—it would have been more natural if she simply ran upstairs, only he needed to hide—but it's no surprise that the conspiracy had spread to them . . . and their nerves must have been strained. I almost saw them walking up from one step to the next step, she first, he behind her, feeling with their feet to keep the creaking to a minimum. I felt bitter. Wasn't this sneaking together a poor surrogate for another sneaking, a hundred-fold more desirable, when she would have been the goal of his sneaking steps? . . . and yet their goal at this moment—not so much Siemian as the killing of him—was no less carnal, sinful, and hot with love, and their sneaking was no less strained. . . . Oh! It creaked once more! Youth was approaching. It was inexpressibly delightful, for under their feet a horrible deed was transforming itself into a blossoming deed, and it was like a breath of fresh air. . . . However . . . this sneaking youth, what was it like, was it pure, was it truly fresh and simple and natural or innocent? No. It was for "the older ones," if those two had forced their way into this affair it was for us, obligingly, to endear themselves to us, to flirt with us a bit . . . and my maturity "for" youth was to meet on Simian's body with their youth "for" maturity—there you have it, what a rendezvous!

Yet there was happiness in it—and pride—and what pride!—and something more, something like vodka—the fact that, in agreement with us, with our whispering into their ear, and actually from their need to serve us, they were taking a risk—and they were thus stealthily sneaking!—they were thus setting about a crime! It was heavenly! It was amazing! In it lay hidden the most fascinating of the world's beauties! Lying on my bed, I was utterly beside myself at the thought that both of us, Fryderyk and I, were an inspiration to those feet—oh, creaking again, now much closer, now silent, silence ensued, I thought they had perhaps broken down, who knows, perhaps, seduced by their sneaking together, they had turned away from their goal and turned toward each other, and now, in an embrace, they forgot everything because they were after their forbidden bodies! In the dark. On the stairs. Breathless. It could be. Really . . . really? Yet no, new creaking announces that my hopes were in vain, nothing changed, they continue walking on up the stairs—it turned out that my hope was utterly, but utterly, in vain, totally out of the question, out of their style. They were too young. Too young. Too young for this! So they had to reach Siemian and kill him. Then I wondered (for it was again silent on the stairs) whether their courage had failed them, perhaps she has caught his hand and is pulling it down, what if the tremendous burden of their task has suddenly appeared to them, its crushing weight, this "to kill"? What if they saw it and became scared? No! Never! This too was out of the question. And for the same reasons. The precipice attracted them because they could jump over it—their lightness strove toward the most bloody undertakings because they were changing this into something else—and their approach to a crime was actually an annihilation of crime, by carrying it out they were annihilating it.

Creaking. Their marvelous illegality, the lightly sneaking sin (boyish-girlish) . . . I almost saw their feet in secret unison, their parted lips, I heard their illicit breathing. I thought about Fryderyk, who was catching the same sounds from downstairs, from the hallway where he had his assigned post, I thought about Vaclav, I saw them all together with Hipolit, with Madame Maria, and with Siemian, who was probably, just like me, lying on his bed—and I breathed in the flavor of virgin crime, of youthful sin. . . . Knock, knock, knock.

Knock, knock, knock!

Knocking. That was she, knocking on Siemian's door.

It is here that my account actually ends. The ending was . . . too smooth and . . . too lightning fast . . . too nimble and easy for me to be able to tell it in a sufficiently believable manner. I will limit myself to stating the facts.

I heard her voice: "It's me." A key turned in Siemian's lock, the door opened, a blow followed, and there was the fall of a body that must have tumbled flat onto the floor. I think the boy used the knife twice more, to leave nothing to chance. I ran into the corridor. Karol shone a flashlight. Siemian lay on the floor, there was blood when we turned him over.

"It's done," Karol said.

Yet the face was grotesquely bound in a kerchief, as if he had a toothache . . . it was not Siemian . . . and it wasn't until a few seconds passed that we realized: Vaclav!

Vaclav instead of Siemian, on the floor, dead. But Siemian too was dead—on the bed, that is—he lay on the bed with a knife wound in his side, his nose nestled in a pillow.

We turned on the light. I watched this, full of eerie misgivings. This . . . this didn't seem one hundred percent real. Too neatly arranged—too easy! I don't know whether I'm expressing it clearly enough, I want to say that it couldn't really be this way, because a suspiciously proper arrangement was inherent in this solution . . . as in a fairy tale, as in a fairy tale. . . . This is what must have happened: Vaclav, right after supper, managed to force his way into Siemian's room through the door connecting their rooms. He killed him. It went smoothly. Then he waited for Henia and Karol's arrival and opened the door. He arranged everything so they would kill him. Smoothly. To make sure, he turned the light off and bound his face in a kerchief—so that he wouldn't be recognized right off.

The ghastliness of my divided consciousness: because the tragic brutality of these corpses, their bloody truth, was too heavy a fruit of a tree too easily bent! Two inert corpses—two killers! As if an idea, deathly final, had been pierced right through by recklessness . . .

We retreated from the room into the hallway. They watched. Saying nothing.

We heard someone running up the stairs. Fryderyk. Upon seeing Vaclav he stopped short. He beckoned to us—we didn't know what it meant. He pulled a knife out of his pocket, held it for a moment in the air, then threw it to the ground. . . . The knife was covered with blood.

"Józek," he said. "Józek. Here he is."

Fryderyk was innocent! He was innocent! He was beaming with innocent naïveté! I looked at our little couple. They were smiling. As the young do when faced with the difficulty of extricating themselves from a predicament. And for a second, they and we, in our catastrophe, looked into one another's eyes.

References

Stanisław Barańczak

Ocalone w tłumaczniu (*Saved in Translation: Sketches on the Craft of Translating Poetry*), Poznań, a5, 1992.

Personal communications.

Bartoszyński, Kazimierz

Kosmos i antynomie (Cosmos and Antinomies) in Pamiętnik Literacki, Warsaw, 1978.

Boyers, Robert

Gombrowicz's Cosmos: the Clinical Fiction as Novel, in Human Inquiries, Summer-Fall, 1971.

Aspects of the Perverse in Gombrowicz's "Pornografia", in Salmagundi, Fall, 1971.

Clues that Lead Nowhere—the Impudent Witold Gombrowicz, in *Harper's,* 2006.

Editorial Sudamericana

Ferdydurke, Spanish translation (Witold Gombrowicz et al.), 1964.

Fenigsen, Richard
Personal communications.

Gombrowicz, Witold
Diary (in Polish), Wydawnictwo Literackie, Kraków, 1988.
Testament, Rozmowy z Dominique de Roux (in Polish) (*A Kind of Testament*), Wydawnictwo Literackie, 1999.

Głowiński, Michał
Parodia konstruktywna (*O "Pornografii" Gombrowicza*), Państwowe Wydawnictwo Naukowe, Warsaw, 1973.
"Ferdydurke" Witolda Gombrowicza, Wydawnictwa Szkolne i Pedagogiczne, Warsaw, 1991.

Hamilton, Alastair
Pornografia, English translation, 1966.

Jarniewicz, Jerzy
"Nalazło, przylazło, oblazło i wlazło, czyli Ferdydurke znowu po angielsku" (in Polish) (*"It came over, crawled over, crept in and over, in other words Ferdydurke in English again"*), in Literatura na Świecie 1–2/2005, p. 369–380.
Personal communication.

Jarzębski, Jerzy
Podgladanie Gombrowicza (in Polish) (*Spying on Gombrowicz*), Wydawnictwo Literackie, Kraków, 2000.
Personal communications.

Libera, Antoni
"*Kosmos, wizja życia—wizja wszechświata*" (in Polish) (*Cosmos, Vision of Life—Vision of Universe*) in Twórczość, 1974.

Markowski, Michał Paweł

Czarny nurt—Gombrowicz, świat, literature (in Polish), (*Black Undertow-Gombrowicz, World, Literature*), Wydawnictwo Literackie, Kraków, 2004.

Personal communication.

Mosbacher, Eric

Ferdydurke, English translation, 1961.

Cosmos, English translation, 1966.

Okopień-Sławińska, Aleksandra

Wielkie bergowanie czyli hipoteza jedności "Kosmosu" (*Great Berging or the Hypothesis of the Unity of "Cosmos"*) written c.1974.

Sédir, George

Ferdydurke, French translation, 1973.